*Wolf Chasm*

Angela Dorsey

# Wolf Chasm

Typeset by Roberta L. Melzl
Editor: Bobbie Chase
Printed in Germany, 2009

ISBN: 978-1-934983-23-2

Stabenfeldt, Inc.
225 Park Avenue South
New York, NY 10003
www.pony4kids.com

*Available exclusively through PONY.*

Clare ran from the house, slamming the front door behind her. It made a soft thud and she stomped back, outraged at the stupid door, at the stupid rug that must've stopped it from closing, at her stupid mom, and even at stupid Mr. Davis.

She shoved the door open, kicked the rug out of the way, then closed the door again as hard as she could. This time it made a satisfying crash, its window rattling with the impact.

She stormed around the back of the house and up the hill to the steep-roofed barn. How could her mom have kept her terrible news a secret? And Mr. Davis had been in on it the whole time!

It was bad enough that they weren't ever coming back to Mr. Davis's ranch in the Yukon Territory. It was bad enough that they had to leave the north and move to the stupid Okanogan. But that she would never see her loyal Smokey again? That was unbearable.

Clare reached the big barn and raced down the center aisle. Smokey heard her footsteps and his long brown face appeared over the top of his stall door. His chocolate coat glimmered and his star and snip shone bright in the barn's subdued lighting. His mane and ear tips appeared as black as ebony.

Clare bit her lip hard and tried to keep from sobbing as

her beautiful best friend struck at his stall door with his front hoof and neighed, sounding overjoyed to see her – and desperate to get out of the suffocating barn. All the other horses had been gone for at least an hour. She opened the door to the stall and slipped inside.

"It's just no fair," she whispered, losing the battle with her tears. She threw her arms around the bay gelding's neck. "Mom hates us. She wants to destroy our lives."

Smokey turned his head and snuffled Clare's straw-colored hair, making her cry harder. She rubbed her face on his long, silky mane, then slowly sank to the straw and leaned on his front legs. She couldn't bear the thought of never seeing Smokey again. It already took all her strength to say goodbye to him every autumn when she and her mom left the ranch, and that was with the knowledge that she'd be back the next spring when Mr. Davis started his summer business of taking tourists horseback riding out on the tundra. More than anything, Clare hated goodbyes, and especially those that lasted forever. They hurt far too much.

And it made no sense to her either. Clare was sure her mom looked forward to coming north too, and that she liked being the cook at the ranch. So why did she say they weren't coming back? A sliver of regret jagged Clare's thoughts. She hadn't heard anything after those first fateful words, and moments later she'd run from the house, overcome with fear and anger. Maybe she should have stayed to listen. Then at least she'd know what excuse her mom had. Not that it would make her feel any better. Not that it would change anything.

Smokey nickered and Clare looked up at him. "I'm not

coming back, Smokes," she said, a hard edge to her voice. "Ever. She won't let me."

Fresh tears coursed down her cheeks. At the very least, her mom should have told her sooner. That way she might have spent even more time with Smokey. They could've gone for longer rides every day. She would have slept in his stall every night. But no. Instead her mom had waited until the very last minute – less than a week left!

Smokey touched Clare's hair again, then reached out and jostled the stall door latch with his muzzle. Obviously, he wanted out, either for a ride or to the pasture. Clare knew he'd never been the kind of horse that enjoyed stalls. He even liked the stars over his head while he slept.

Smokey touched the latch again, then stared at her with his dark, understanding eyes. He knew what she needed too – a long ride.

"You're right, Smokes," Clare said, pushing her hair out of her eyes. "Let's get out of here."

She reached over the door, grabbed Smokey's mechanical hackamore from the wall outside the stall, and slipped it on his head. Then she opened the door wide and ran before him as he trotted from the stall and down the aisle. They stopped at the open barn doors and she looked toward the house. Her mom hadn't come out yet, but Clare knew she would. She always came, after giving Clare ample time to cool down. It was part of their ritual, the way they made things better after a fight.

But this time, there was no way her mom could make things better. This was the worse thing she'd ever done, and Clare didn't want to talk to her now, or possibly ever again.

7

Separating her and Smokey was so heartless that Clare could hardly believe her mother was really doing it – it was like she was a different person than the one Clare thought she knew.

She heard the distant thud of a closing door. Her mom!

"Oh no," she whispered and hurried to Smokey's side. "Down, boy," she said and tapped his neck. Obediently, the horse lowered his neck and Clare flung herself across the black mane. When Smokey raised his head, she slid onto his withers, swung her right leg over his back, then leaned forward. "Let's go, Smokes."

The gelding didn't hesitate. He leapt into a canter. Together they raced across the stable yard and along the trail leading out onto the wild tundra.

"Clare!"

She leaned farther over Smokey's back and encouraged him to run faster.

"Clare!" Already her mom's voice was fading in the distance.

New tears sprung to her eyes. Her mom didn't understand anything. Didn't she know that Clare loved the north, with its harsh beauty and amazing wildness, with its landscape so stark and lone and untouched that it made your heart ache just to see it? But most of all, didn't she know how Smokey meant everything to Clare?

How cruel could she be?

With a whine, Snowfall flopped down to lie panting
beneath a willow bush. She licked at her worn forepaws,
then laid her ears back as her stomach growled. Hunger
was like a rat inside of her, gnawing at her insides, at her
energy, at her wellbeing. There was no good hunting left
near the cave. They'd been here too long. The hares and
mice they'd been surviving on had either been eaten or
had moved on. Just as she and her pack needed to do –
move on to new hunting grounds. Move on to find the
caribou. Move on to become healthier and fatter before
winter came to swallow the land.

She looked up at the ridge before her. How she longed
to gather her pups and walk away. This protected place
had become a cage to them – but they couldn't leave. If
she and the pups left to new hunting grounds, Avalanche,
her brother, would not survive. He wasn't strong enough
to come with them, and without the few morsels she was
able to bring him every now and then, he would die.

Yet she had to do something, and soon. With every
day that passed, the pups grew thinner and weaker, and
so did she. Every day she smelled the scent of winter on
the air, just a little closer. If they didn't leave soon, they
would all face extinction. That was a fact. But how could
she leave her brother behind?

The silver wolf growled low in her throat. This was all

because of the human. If it hadn't killed her mate, Ranger, if it hadn't shot Avalanche and wounded him, they would all be happy and healthy. The pups would be bouncing about being carefree wolf pups, learning about the world instead of huddling in the back of a dark cave, watching their uncle waste away. And worse, wasting away themselves.

Starving. They were all slowly starving.

Snowfall rose to her feet. She had a decision to make soon: leave with the pups and let Avalanche die, or stay and hope that large game came to their canyon. There were no other options, and the longer she waited to decide, the weaker they would all become. One wolf couldn't catch enough to feed six, especially when the hares were gone, the mice almost hunted out.

She had tried to catch a fish in the river, but only succeeded in almost freezing to death in the current that caught her up. Just before losing her ability to swim in the cold water, she'd reached shore. However, luck was with her two days later when she'd been able to steal a morsel of a fish away from an eagle, and that eagle might still be around. Maybe she should check the riverbank first today.

The silver wolf trotted along the gravel bar, her eyes roving from the grass and willows on the bank to the stream rushing past on her other side. No sign of the eagle or any fish carcasses. But she couldn't give up, no matter how hungry she was, no matter how tired. Her pups depended on her. Avalanche depended on her. She was their only hope. As long as she was able to draw breath, she would do all she could.

11

Smokey galloped along the trail that Mr. Davis used when he took tourists out on horseback. His head and tail were high and he had a rolling spring to his gait. Obviously, he was enjoying himself immensely. Clare felt her tears blow away in the wind created by his gallop and their remnants dry on her face. She kept her elbows close to her side for warmth. She'd left without a coat and the wind was chilly. She could even smell autumn in the air, but there was no way she was going to go back for her jacket.

She pulled Smokey to a quick stop at the top of a hill. The tundra spread out around her, stunning in the morning light. The vegetation seemed to glow, and here and there Clare noticed the yellow and orange of fall touching the alpine plants. She felt another flash of rage – reminders were everywhere. She couldn't escape them. They always left in the fall. She always said goodbye to her dear Smokey, but this time she wouldn't be coming back. She stroked his silky neck. What would he think next year when she didn't return? That she'd betrayed him? Abandoned him? That she'd died?

"Clare!" The shout was distant. Clare shaded her eyes as she scanned the open spaces for movement. There they were – Mr. Davis and his tourists, four of them this time: two adults and two kids. A family.

She quickly reined Smokey to the east, toward the rising

sun. The last thing she wanted was to see Mr. Davis right now. He had betrayed her almost as much as her mom – he could have told her there would be no returning next year. And it could even be his fault that they weren't coming back. Maybe he'd fired her mom, as ridiculous as that sounded. Her mom was an awesome cook. Clare scowled as she rode. She didn't want to think anything good about her mom right now.

She heard another far off shout and looked back at Mr. Davis and his group. He was waving to her. Instead of waving back, Clare asked her gelding to canter away.

She inhaled deeply as they swept over the tundra, Smokey weaving around brush and obstacles as surefooted as a caribou. The sharp air entered her lungs over and over, slowly and surely uncluttering her mind – and when she could think clearly again, she knew just where she was going to go: the Chasm. She'd always wanted to go there, but both Mr. Davis and her mom had forbidden it. They'd said it was too far, too remote, too dangerous. Too many bad things could happen. But this day couldn't get any worse.

And this would probably be her last long ride, her last chance to see that wild remote canyon, her last long day out on the tundra with Smokey for the rest of her life. If she didn't go today, she never would, because as soon as she got home, she was going to be grounded for sure. She'd yelled too many mean and horrid things at her mom before slamming that door.

She reined Smokey in the direction of the distant canyon. She had only ridden within sight of its steep walls twice, but both times it completely intrigued her. The first time she'd noted how narrow the Chasm was and how choked with willows and stunted trees. She'd admired the good-sized river spewing from its mouth. The second time she'd brought binoculars and was both thrilled and frightened to view a grizzly fishing in the river, its massive hump rising above the willows whenever it would bring a fish ashore to eat.

A shiver coursed down her back. What if the bear was back this year? Maybe she should reconsider. Maybe she should ride to the muskeg swamp and look for foxes instead. Or climb the small mountain near their home.

No. Not today. Nothing tame today, she decided. If she was forced to leave here forever, she wanted a wild adventure to see her off. Maybe not so wild as to include a bear, but she would keep a sharp eye out and go somewhere else if she saw one fishing. She had lots of time today because she wasn't going to get home until after dark. That would teach her mom and Mr. Davis a lesson.

Crouch. Leap. Plunge. Sharp sedge grass in mouth, cutting her tongue, slicing her gums. But she had it – another mouse!

Snowfall crunched down quick, ending its short life, and trotted to where she left the first mouse she'd caught that day. Now she had two – for four pups and her injured brother. She couldn't stop yet.

She dropped the tiny body to lie with the first, then lay down to rest yet again. She kept her paw on the two mice, just in case someone else was hungry enough to brave approaching her. The scent of them wafted into her nostrils. They would be so delicious. She could almost taste them.

She turned her head and looked toward the river. She couldn't eat them. No. No. Her pups needed them far more than she did, and so did Avalanche.

A hawk cried overhead and she looked up. The bird of prey was hunting too. Scanning the undergrowth for mice. Maybe if she followed him, watched him hunt, she could pounce on his find before he could dive to the earth.

Snowfall rose up, took the two mice in her jaws to carry, and trotted after the hawk as it circled above her. It shrieked again. Loudly. And this time when she looked up, it flew away. It had guessed her plan.

15

A rustle in the undergrowth! Another mouse? Or a hare?

Moving slowly, Snowfall dropped her pups' dinner to the ground, silently scratched some dirt on top of them, then crept toward the rustling noise.

Clare pulled Smokey to a halt when the Chasm came into sight. It was still distant, at least four miles away, but she could see the flash of the river reflecting sunlight as it flowed from between the canyon walls. Beside the river, willow bushes and scrub conifers grew, then the sides of the Chasm rose steeply to become crumbling rock and barely clinging shrubs. It looked so intriguing and mystical. Even magical. She could just imagine it as being a hidden fairy kingdom.

And there were no dark dots moving by the river that she could see – no bears. So far, so good.

She asked Smokey to walk, stroking his hot neck as they moved closer to the canyon mouth. "I'm so mad at them, Smokes," she murmured. "I can't believe I only have one more week here, that I'll never see you again after that – it's not fair. How can she decide something like that without asking me? I'm not a little kid anymore but it's like I have no say at all. I just have to do what she tells me and it makes me just want to scream and scream and scream at her."

Clare chewed her bottom lip. She sounded so bitter, even to herself. Smokey didn't need to hear that. She leaned over his mane as he walked and sighed deeply. "But most of all, really, I'm sad," she whispered and let her tears mingle with the light sweat glistening his neck. "I can't lose you too. I just can't."

Smokey stopped, then nickered and turned his head to

17

look at her with compassionate eyes. He might not know what was exactly wrong, but he knew she was upset and was sad with her. He was her best friend, her truest ally. She could always count on him – but after next week, he wasn't going to be there to count on. And he wouldn't be able to count on her either. That thought was the most painful of all.

Clare buried her face in her hands. The more she thought about things, the more she felt certain that Smokey would think she was dead – and she knew that terrible feeling. Her dad had died when she was a little girl and she still missed him. She could hardly remember his face, except from pictures, but she remembered how he smelled. She remembered him picking her up and holding her high in the air and that she didn't feel the least bit afraid because she knew he'd never let her fall. She remembered the love-light in his eyes. Then one day, he disappeared. She heard tearful words like "heart attack" and "gone suddenly" but the words meant nothing. What did imprint on her little-girl brain was that her dad never came home again. And that's what would happen to Smokey. He wouldn't understand and he'd wait for her, and then when she didn't come home and didn't come home and didn't come home, he'd eventually give up, just like she did.

There was no way she wanted Smokey to go through that misery. She had to stop their separation from happening, for both him, and for herself. Even though she'd know Smokey wasn't dead, even though Mr. Davis would tell her how he was doing if she phoned him, she couldn't bear to lose another whom she loved.

But how was she to stop her mom from taking her away?

The rustling creature was gone by the time Snowfall reached the spot where it had been, but she knew what it was – an arctic hare. Its scent was a heady perfume in her nose and mouth. But the wild rabbits were so fast. It was probably uncatchable by now. And it would take so much energy to chase, energy she didn't really have.

Her nose twitched and she flicked her tail.

If, however, she was able to find and catch it, it would provide a satisfying meal for her pups, plus she'd have the mice to give to Avalanche.

She would hunt it.

Snowfall trotted back to her two mice and glanced hastily about. She saw no one who might steal her catch. She pawed extra dirt over the two, then lowered her head to sniff the ground. The main scent here was wolf – herself – not mouse. They should be safe.

Weakly, she turned and trotted back to where the hare had been, her ears perked. Her sharp eyes searched for movement and she inhaled the wild creature's scent, then started to track it. If only she could catch it – the hare would be such a boon to her desperate family. For one day, her hunting would be done and she could rest. For one day, her pups wouldn't go hungry. And Avalanche? Well, it was true that two mice weren't enough for a grown wolf like him, especially when he was injured, but two mice were better than nothing.

Rage rose inside her again in an unstoppable flood. If only her brother hadn't been hurt by the human. If he were well, none of them would be starving. They'd be following the caribou herds, hunting together and teaching the pups to hunt. The human had destroyed all that. By killing Ranger, her mate, and injuring Avalanche, the human was slowly killing them all.

She growled. If the human were there right now, she'd attack without hesitation. She'd rip it to shreds – that was the only suitable revenge for the life of her mate.

Ranger, iron gray and powerful, the alpha male in their small pack, had growled a warning to Snowfall and Avalanche when he'd first seen the human riding past them on a big brown creature. At first the human hadn't seen them, but then it looked in their direction, stopped the brown creature, put a long stick to its shoulder and pointed it toward them. An unbelievable *BOOM!* echoed around them.

Ranger fell.

Snowfall had run a few yards away before she noticed that Ranger hadn't jumped up to follow them. Without thinking, she raced back to his side. Avalanche followed her. Ranger seemed to be sleeping, his eyes closed. Snowfall licked his face, trying to rouse him, but he didn't even twitch. Then she saw the blood on his side. She noticed that his ribs no longer moved up and down in their steady, perfect rhythm. He wasn't breathing.

Another *BOOM!* and Avalanche cried out beside her.

It was then that she realized that the strange sound was causing the injuries – and the noise was coming from the human sitting on the brown creature.

It had killed her mate! It had injured her brother!

Confused at how to fight a noise, she and Avalanche fled. However, within minutes, Avalanche began to have trouble running. Then even walking was difficult. In the end, he dragged himself the last of the distance to their den by his front paws, his back legs trailing useless behind him. Once inside, he inched to the back of the cave and tumbled down the slope at the back. He'd been there ever since.

Snowfall's hackles stuck straight up as she trotted along, her nose to the ground to smell the hare's passing. Remembering Ranger's death day fueled the hatred inside her heart. How she wanted to fight that human creature, hurt it, kill it! Just as it had killed Ranger.

But for now, she needed to concentrate on hunting. For now, finding enough food for them all was more important than getting revenge on a human who wasn't even there. For now.

A brown form darted from the willows ahead and Snowfall was after it like a flash. The hare! She had to catch it!

The wind came up when they were less than a mile from the Chasm. It swept across the treeless space like a grizzly was on its tail. Clare wrapped her arms around herself. Once more she wished she'd thought to bring a jacket. Her shirt, though fleece, was no match for this frigid gale. Autumn had definitely arrived, quickly and almost overnight, like it always did. Winter would be along shortly. And then there would be seven or eight months of cold and snow, depending on the year.

But she wouldn't be worrying about that ever again. She wouldn't be watching the calendar next spring, counting down the days until they could come back to the ranch. She'd never run out to the pasture again, calling Smokey's name. She'd never get to see him gallop toward her, neighing the whole while, as if asking her what took her so long this year. Anger flushed Clare's face again, and for a moment she forgot the cold. This was all her mom's fault!

As they drew nearer the Chasm, the height of land rising to her left seemed to break the wind a bit. In fact, from the direction it was blowing, Clare wondered if there would be any wind inside the canyon at all. She hoped not. Her teeth were already chattering, but she didn't want to turn back now.

When they reached the first of the scrubby evergreen trees, she stopped Smokey. The trees were further evidence that the canyon was protected from the prevailing winds.

There weren't any trees out on the open land, because the wind and winter storms kept most of the vegetation to a low stubble. Here though the canyon protected them enough that they could grow in gnarly shapes.

She peered ahead through the brush and tree trunks that choked the entrance to the Chasm. "I don't see any bears," she said to the gelding and shivered. "Do you?"

Smokey's stance was relaxed and he looked around with bright, interested eyes, then stepped forward without her asking. Obviously, he saw nothing dangerous – no grizzlies. In fact, he seemed excited to be exploring someplace new and different. He wove through the trees that grew more numerous as they walked between the rocky walls.

Clare relaxed her hugging hold on her arms, relieved. She'd been right. There was no wind inside the Chasm. It was the perfect place to ride today.

The evergreens diminished and willows thickened as they neared the bank of the river flowing down the center of the canyon. Smokey pushed his way through the chest-high brush to the river's edge, then turned to follow a wild animal trail that ran alongside it.

"Good thinking, Smokes," said Clare. She looked at the clear water running beside them. The river was a small one, not big enough to roar, but it certainly did more than tinkle. The sound was a happy one as the current splashed and eddied and tumbled over rocks, swirled in big pools. The sky reflected on its shimmering surface, tinting the water with light blue ripples. She could even see long flashes of silver, contorted by the moving water – fish in the stream. How beautiful!

For the first time all day, Clare felt her heart lighten, but then she remembered why she was angry and the feeling twisted into something even darker than before. She would never be back here again.

A flash of bright blue made her gasp and she pulled Smokey to a quick stop. A Mountain Bluebird landed on the willows to her left. He lifted his beak into the air and warbled, then shook his wings and was off again, a flying patch of sky skimming over the brush. Finally, he disappeared into the branches of a nearby tree. Smokey shook his ebony mane and snorted.

"So pretty," Clare said, still awed by the beautiful bird. She didn't often see Mountain Bluebirds so far north. This canyon really was special. A gift. It was like the north was trying to give her something wonderful, something priceless to remember before she had to leave it forever.

She frowned. Just for a few minutes she wanted to forget that this was her last week. She couldn't enjoy this day to the max if she was feeling angry and upset and sad.

"Let's go, Smokey," she said and touched the bay's chocolate sides with her heels. The gelding stepped out eagerly, his ears forward. He was so unaware, so innocent. He totally trusted that her love for him would bring her back. And she always had come back before, every other year of his life. Her breath caught in her throat.

Here she was thinking about it again! For Smokey's sake, she had to at least pretend nothing was wrong. She had to make sure they had this one last wonderful day: exploring new places, riding along a beautiful creek, watching bluebirds, and who knew what else. That would be her parting gift to him, and to herself; she'd give them both a perfect day to remember for the rest of their lives. But to do that, she needed to control her anger and sadness – if that was remotely possible.

Snowfall raced through the willows. The wild rabbit ran, panting, just a few feet in front of her, but no matter how hard she tried, Snowfall couldn't gain on it. It almost seemed as if the hare was playing with her – not wanting to get caught, of course, but not wanting to expend too much energy running from her. Normally she would have given up after a few strides, but she was desperate. There was no other game around, other than the odd mouse.

The hare's rump appeared and disappeared in front of her as they darted through the vegetation. Now and then, she thought she was gaining on it, but then, the next time she'd see it, it would be farther away again. She pushed herself harder and gained a few feet on the hare, but then it noticed how close she was and leapt into the air, kicked out with its powerful back legs, and easily pulled away from her, disappearing into the undergrowth.

Snowfall tried to follow the sounds of its passage through the bush, but the noise was subtle, much quieter than the noise she made herself, and soon she lost track of it. She slowed to a trot, then a walk, then collapsed on the ground, breathing hard.

The hare had avoided her so easily. Snowfall whined. She knew what that meant. She'd lost too much strength.

She was no longer fast enough to catch a hare, and this had been a young one too, not as fast as the adult hares. She was too weak to catch much more than mice – which meant that her family was doomed.

She could feed herself, become stronger, and let them get even hungrier as she gained strength to hunt more food, or she could continue on the same path and catch mice for them, refrain from eating herself, and eventually become too weak to hunt.

Either way, her pups were going to starve.

Anger colored her vision once again, then faded away. She didn't even have the energy for that anymore. Snowfall rose to her feet. She needed to get moving. She would continue feeding the pups first, enough to keep them alive. Avalanche second, so he could get well. And she herself would eat third. Or in other words, wouldn't eat at all, because she would never catch enough to feed herself after the others.

But this way was the best, because it would keep her pups alive the longest. It would give them the best chance, and that was the most important thing.

Slowly, she trotted back to where she'd buried the two mice. Just three more and she could return to the cave with one for each of them. Then she could rest.

Smokey stopped short and looked to the left, his head high
and his ears at attention. He'd heard something.

"What is it, boy?" asked Clare, patting his shoulder.
Smokey was the best horse she'd ever known for noticing
danger. If he thought they should get away, Clare certainly
wouldn't stop him. However, Smokey merely bobbed his
head to further loosen the reins and stepped forward. He
wanted to investigate whatever he'd heard. Clare urged him
on. She was curious too.

The gelding shoved his way through the brush and then
walked between more scattered scrubby trees. There was
no path to follow here and Clare kept low over his withers to avoid being pushed from his back by branches. The
horse was careful to not walk too close to the trunks – he
knew to keep her knees from smacking into them.
Finally, they reached an open space. The ground rose before them in a chaotic tumble of rocks to meet the cliff that
was the left side of the canyon.

Clare pulled Smokey to a halt and scanned the area
in front of them. It looked perfectly ordinary. What had
Smokey noticed? She held her breath and listened. Nothing. But the horse was still standing at attention, looking up
at the cliff before them. Her gaze followed his – and then
she saw it. A dark slit in the rock. A cave! How cool! There
was even a faint trail leading up to the opening.

Was there something in the cave? Was that what Smokey heard?

"Should we go investigate, Smokes?" asked Clare, feeling reckless. Surely, there couldn't be anything too dangerous in the cave. It was far too soon for bears to hibernate. They would be at the rivers, scooping up as many fish as possible with their burly front legs and long claws, then carrying them to the banks to devour them. This was the time of year when they tried to gain as much weight as they could, so they could survive the long winter, asleep in their dens. And the wolf packs would be following the caribou herds. What else could hurt her while she was on her sturdy horse's back?

Nothing.

She urged Smokey forward and he eagerly began to climb the scree slope. Maybe she'd find a lynx near the cave. That would be so amazing! Lynxes were terribly shy creatures and in all the summers she'd spent in the north, she'd never seen one.

The cave mouth grew larger as they approached and despite her anticipation of seeing what was inside, Clare shivered. What if she was wrong and there was a pack of wolves, a bear, or even a wolverine watching her from inside the cave? She'd forgotten about the danger of wolverines. They were one of the fiercest predators of all. Mr. Davis once told her a story of watching a sixty-pound wolverine hunt and kill a one-thousand-pound moose. That was as large as Smokey, and she knew that moose could be ferocious too. For such a large animal to be killed by a small predator seemed an impossible feat, but Clare knew it wasn't. Though small, wolverines were one of the strongest, meanest creatures alive.

"Hey in there!" she yelled as they approached, hoping to see something move behind the darkness. If she had an idea of the size of the creature inside – if there was one at all – she would know what to do. If the noise Smokey had heard had been an owl, or a ground squirrel, or even just the wind, there was nothing to worry about. Or maybe he'd simply seen the empty cave in the distance and wanted to explore it. She knew that she definitely did.

As they drew near, Clare paid as much attention to Smokey's movements as she did to the cave. She knew his subtle actions would tell her more than her own senses about what she could expect inside, because he could see things she couldn't and hear and smell things of which she was totally unaware. He did seem a little on edge, but not much. Not enough to turn around anyway.

He stopped outside the cave and Clare bent over his withers to peer inside. The cave seemed to be one large stony chamber, although it was possible that the darker areas at the back concealed openings to deeper chambers. One thing was for sure, it was the ideal den for something. And it did seem empty – perfect for exploring! However, she'd have to dismount. The entrance wasn't high enough for her to ride Smokey inside.

Clare slid from Smokey's bare back, then lifted the looped hackamore reins over his head. "Come on, buddy," she murmured and led him forward. "Let's check it out."

Smokey snorted softly and held his ground.

Clare turned back to him. "You can stay here if you want, Smokes. I'll just be a minute." She stroked the white snip on his nose, then turned back to the cave and walked inside. This time he followed her through the low doorway.

Clare walked to the middle of the chamber and stopped. "This is so cool," she murmured as she turned a complete circle. "I wonder if we're the first horse and human to be in here. I bet you're the first horse, anyway."

She looked up at the high rock ceiling, patched in daylight and shadow, then let her gaze travel to the back of the cave. The ceiling sloped down there, probably making it too low for Smokey. Clare walked along the right side of the cave, her free hand dragging along the rock face, loosening dirt and stray pebbles.

Wouldn't it be cool if she found ancient cave drawings in here? The wall on this side was too crumbly and rough, but... she looked to the other side of the chamber. It was the same on both sides. In fact, on the left side, rocks lay on the floor where they'd fallen free from the wall. But maybe it was smooth enough for cave drawings at the back of the cave, deeper inside the mountain – and even if she couldn't find any, she should try to make some of her own. That would be so cool. Then when she was grown up and came back to the north, she could come here to find her own drawings. She could even draw pictures that told of how her mom forced her away from their summer home, of how her mom was so cruel as to separate Clare and Smokey. It would be a permanent record of her grief.

She led Smokey toward the rear of the cave, thinking they could go only so far before the lowered ceiling stopped them, but as she moved closer to the back, the floor became lower too. Then it dropped off into the darkness, a steep decline. Clare stopped at the edge, peered off into the gloom and waited for her eyes to adjust. It looked like another chamber waited at the bottom of the slope.

"Stay, buddy," Clare murmured and dropped his reins. She'd never regretted the time she'd taken to teach Smokey to ground-tie. It had come in handy dozens of times over the years and in some ways was the most valuable thing she'd ever taught him, especially in this land of few trees.

She slid down the slope, sending loose rocks tumbling before her. When she reached the flat area, she stopped. The stillness at the back of the cave was so thick that she could hear her own breathing. It was as if the sounds from outside, the birdsong, the wind, the rustling vegetation, the river, couldn't reach this far inside the mountain.

The wall higher up was still illuminated from the cave mouth, but down low where Clare stood, the darkness reigned. She saw some massive lumps in front of her that had to be boulders – and behind them? Utter blackness. The back of the cave? Or tunnels that went deeper into the earth?

It was too weird, how she could hear her own breathing so clearly. Maybe there were other things she could hear that were unusual. Like an underground river? Or ghosts from the past, she thought and smiled as she leaned forward, holding her breath to listen.

The breathing sound didn't stop.

Clare's eyes widened and she gasped, momentarily hiding the sound of *someone else breathing in the darkness!* She spun around to lunge up the short slope. Smokey stepped back, wild-eyed, as she charged toward him and grabbed his reins. She spun around again, pressing against his shoulder, and stared back the way she'd come. Who had she heard? What was there?

Taking her courage in hand, she held her breath again to listen. There was no sound, other than a bird singing outside and Smokey's calm shiftings. Could her own breathing have been echoing back to her? Immediately she felt better. That totally made sense.

"Stupid, that's what I am," she said, her heart still thudding in her chest. She turned to give the gelding a hug.

A rattle of stones came from her left and she turned her head, expecting to see tiny rocks sliding down the crumbly cave wall.

Instead, a fluffy bundle of gray fur rocketed from behind one of the rocks, tumbled past her, and disappeared down the slope.

A wolf pup! How cute!

Without considering her actions, Clare hurried back to the edge of the slope and searched the darkness below – but the wolf pup, with his dark gray fur, was well hidden in the shadows.

Where was its family? Clare inhaled sharply and backed toward Smokey. "We should go, Smokes," she murmured when she reached the horse. "We don't want to disturb any wild babies. And we don't want to be here when its parents get back."

As if to spur her on, a growl drifted from below. The deep timbre seemed too low to have come from such a small pup and Clare hurried Smokey to the mouth of the cave. She strode through the opening, the horse on her heels – and stopped short.

Massive snowflakes were drifting from the sky. Already the ground was white. How had it happened so quickly? And it was early for the first snowfall. She'd thought they had another couple weeks.

But this is the north, she reminded herself. There can be snowstorms in August.

Clare quickly mounted and reined Smokey toward home. Being mad at her mom and Mr. Davis was one thing, but endangering herself and Smokey was another, and if this snow kept falling, she would be doing just that. She didn't even have a jacket, let alone any survival gear if she was trapped out on the tundra.

At least it didn't matter that she didn't have a compass. Smokey would know the way home, even in a disorienting snowstorm. Now they just had to get there, before the snow got too deep, the day too cold.

Snowfall was three miles from the cave when the snow started. First a flake fell on the bush beside her, and another at her paws, and another on her nose. Then a cloud of swirling white surrounded her.

The silver wolf whimpered. Hunting was over for the day. All prey, both large and small, would be taking shelter. And she had only caught two mice. Only two of her babies would eat today.

Slowly, she turned. How she hated giving up the hunt. But on the other hand, it would be so nice to rest. Back in the cave, she could lie down. She could try to regain some strength – as two of her puppies and Avalanche were further consumed by the hunger that stalked them. But there was no other choice.

She trotted back the way she'd come, moving quickly on her long legs. She kept her head low, her eyes sharp, as she covered ground, just in case she saw movement – but the snow was falling too thick and fast to see much of anything.

She was a mile from the cave when she noticed the strange smell. She raised her head and sniffed deeply. A human! And one of those big creatures – just like the two who had killed Ranger!

A low growl rumbled in her throat and she pulled back her lips in a snarl. What were they doing in her canyon? What evil intentions did they have so close to her home?

Snowfall leapt into a sudden run. Her pups! The human must be after her pups! Killing Ranger wasn't enough for it. It wanted to eliminate her entire family.

The ground sped by beneath her padded paws, and within minutes the cave was before her, swiftly drawing nearer. The smell of human was so strong here that she felt sick – it had found her home!

Her claws scrambled on the rocks as she ran up the slope to the entrance to her den. The scent was nauseating. She burst through the entrance and slid to a halt.

Her pups, where were her pups? And Avalanche?

She dropped the mice to the floor of the cave, and barked once.

A pup yelped from the back of the cave. Aurora! At least one had survived. When the silver gray pup rushed forward to grab one of the mice, Snowfall whined in relief. Then behind her came the other three: Scout, the little dark male who for some reason thought he was the biggest and toughest of the pups; Ice, the light colored male who always gave in to his smaller brother; and Tundra, the medium-gray female who was far too mischievous for her own good.

Scout and Ice reached the second mouse at the same time and a tug of war ensued, until Scout growled and lunged at Ice and the bigger pup released his grip on their meal. Two seconds later, the mouse had been gulped ravenously down. Ice and Tundra could only sniff at the spot where the mice had lain.

Snowfall walked stiff-legged to the back of the cave, her hackles still raised. Avalanche barely raised his head at her approach he was so weak. She sniffed the ground around him – the human creature hadn't come this far.

She looked up at her pups, still sniffing for more food on the cave's higher ground. She'd taught them well. They'd hidden when the intruder came to kill them. They'd kept still and silent and the human creature had gone away.

However, it was too dangerous to keep them here now. She had to move them to another place to keep them hidden. She would take Aurora first – she was the strongest pup, and the one most likely to survive the trek to find a new den. Then when she'd secured a new home, she'd come back for the others.

But first, she had something terrible to do. Snowfall whined. Avalanche may not still be living when she returned from this search for a new den – and even if he was, there was no way he could follow them when she took the last pup.

Before she left, she had to say goodbye to her brother.

Clare huddled as close to Smokey's withers as she could and kept her hands beneath his heavy mane as they rode toward the canyon mouth. She was freezing and they'd hardly started their ride home. It would take at least an hour to get within sight of the ranch, and almost twice that to travel the entire distance.

At least Smokey wasn't suffering too much. His winter coat had started to come in a couple weeks before. It still wasn't thick, but he would definitely be warmer than she on their long ride home.

Snow completely blanketed the ground now, making it appear soft and untouched. As usual when it first snowed, Clare remembered the first time she'd seen snow as a little kid. For some reason, she thought it looked warm and so she ran out into it without a coat or boots. The biting cold was so shocking, all she could do was scream until her dad came to rescue her, laughing all the while. Now, even more than that day, she regretted that snow wasn't warm. It would be such delightful, wonderful stuff then.

Right now, it was anything but delightful. The snowfall was so heavy that the flakes were even building up on the thin willow stems – which meant that as they wove their way through the brush, the snow was coming off onto the two of them, and melting. Clare's jeans were getting wetter and wetter, her legs colder and colder. She could only pray that when they reached the open tundra, they'd find their way dry and clear.

Please, please, she thought and crossed her frigid fingers with difficulty. Smokey's mane wasn't helping nearly enough. Her hands were numb with the cold, which meant the weather was doing more than just snowing. The temperature must be dropping too.

They rode into the trees and for a moment, Clare felt better. The trees stopped some of the snow from falling on them and it was drier beneath the boughs, even though the cold still bit at her through her wet clothes. But then they reached the smaller, more gnarled trees, close to the Chasm opening. The trees offered little protection here. And worse, there was even a touch of wind.

At last they were at the mouth of the Chasm, facing the tundra. Clare didn't need to touch the reins to make Smokey halt. He stopped  on his own, then reached out and struck the ground. His hoof made no sound. The snow completely muffled the impact.

"Are we in trouble or what, Smokes?"

On the open land before them, the wind pushed the snow past in a blinding wall. Clare and Smokey were protected from the storm in the Chasm where, thanks to the narrow opening, the wind couldn't reach them – but to ride out on the tundra would be certain death.

Smokey snorted and backed a step when a whirl of wind came too close, the white flakes caught in its grip creating and destroying a dozen ghosts over and over again in its midst.

"But we have to get home, Smokey." Tears sprung

from Clare's eyes and slid a couple inches down her cheek before they froze.

The gelding turned and started quickly back the way they'd come.

"No, Smokey, we have to go home." Clare pulled back on the reins.

Smokey flexed his neck, but refused to stop. Snow tumbled down the back of Clare's shirt from a branch and she squealed and leaned forward over his neck. Where was he going? Should she turn him back? They were just going to get colder and colder in the canyon – and then when they started across the tundra, they'd be in even worse shape.

"Smokey," she tried one more time. When he didn't even look back at her, she dropped the reins on his neck and shoved her frozen hands back under his mane. Reluctantly, she admitted he was right. It was too dangerous to try to make a run for it across the tundra. It was probably ten times colder out there in the wind, and she was already shivering uncontrollably. It was safer to stay in the canyon and wait for the storm to die down. And it would. It was too early in the year for any snowstorm to last long.

Her legs burned where her wet jeans were touching her skin. She put one numb hand on her thigh. Sure enough, her jeans were frozen. She couldn't even feel the willows scraping against her legs as Smokey hurried through the brush.

A thin tremor came from beneath her – Smokey was starting to shiver too. How was she going to warm them both up?

Her hands were too numb to fit inside her pockets, so she patted the outside. There was a familiar bump there – her penknife. Good. At least, she hadn't forgotten that. But there were no other bumps. No gloves. No hand warmers or matches to light them with – but of course there wouldn't be. She hadn't put any in her pocket before leaving home this morning.

It wasn't until they were halfway back to the cave that she realized that must be where Smokey was headed. It made perfect sense. He knew they needed shelter. Even though there was no wind in the canyon, the temperature was still dropping. Her hair, once wet, was now frozen and hanging in stiff spikes from her head. But even though the cave would keep the snow off them, it wouldn't warm them up. It wouldn't dry her clothes or his body. They would need some source of heat once they reached the cave.

She patted her pocket again – still no matches. But there were other ways to light a fire. She didn't have a mirror to use – and there was no sunlight available anyway to ignite some dry tinder – but maybe she could find some flint somewhere. She could use the under-part of Smokey's mane as the first fuel. It would be the driest. She could cut off a few hairs with her penknife and then strike a spark with the flint that would ignite them, and then she could put on some dry sticks and larger bits of wood. Hopefully, she could find some sticks lying around the cave, otherwise dry wood could be a little hard to find.

Smokey started to climb and Clare looked up. They were already on the scree slope in front of the cave. For a moment, she couldn't breathe. She'd forgotten about the wolf pups. What if their parents had come home? What about the growl she'd heard coming from the darkness? Would a pack of wolves just let her enter their cave and build a fire? She didn't think so.

She swallowed. But she didn't have a choice. *They* didn't have a choice. If they didn't go into the cave, they'd freeze to death. They might anyway, if she couldn't get a fire lit, but if they didn't go inside, they were goners for sure. She could only hope and pray like crazy that the big wolves hadn't come home yet.

Snowfall was at the back of the cave, licking Avalanche's ears, when Ice yipped and then all four pups tumbled down the slope toward her, a bundle of gray, black, and silver. Snowfall whined at them to keep quiet and perked her ears toward the top of the slope. Something was coming near the entrance to their cave. Something heavy!

When Aurora crept toward the sound, Snowfall nipped at her and sent the pup scurrying back with her brothers and sister to press against the cave's back wall. Then with a steely look at them to stay put, Snowfall slunk forward.

It was hard creeping up the slope without sending any pebbles rattling downward, pebbles that would give away their presence to the intruder, but Snowfall was good at stealth. She tested each step before she took it and, bit by bit, made it high enough that she could see over the crest to the cave opening.

The beast was coming closer and closer – she could hear it clearly now – and it seemed too noisy for a bear, though it sounded as heavy. Rocks shifted beneath the snow as it walked and once it stumbled. Then Snowfall heard something that made her blood run cold: the babbling sound that came from humans' funny looking mouths.

She leapt wildly down to where her puppies cowered. She had to save them! She had to hide them from the murderous human!

Her pups caught her panic and whimpered as they crowded behind the only boulder big enough to hide them all. Avalanche merely closed his eyes. He could do nothing to help them, or himself.

Panic-stricken, Snowfall turned again to face the horrible creatures. Though she couldn't see the cave mouth from the bottom of the decline, she could imagine them as they entered the cave. The human might even be the same one that had killed her mate – tall and thin with hair on its face. It would be sitting on the same big brown beast that looked like an un-horned caribou, only taller. The human would have a *BOOM*-stick in its hands and would be ready to use it.

Soon it would search the cave for them – and because there was no good place to hide, it would find them. There was only one way out of the cave, and the human and its deadly stick were between the escape route and them.

It would kill them.

Terror jittered along Snowfall's spine, making her entire body tremble. A mournful howl fought to escape from her jaws, a howl of desperation and defeat and sadness. An apology to Ranger: she hadn't been able to keep their puppies safe. An apology to the puppies themselves: their lives would be too short. And to Avalanche, her brother. She hadn't been able to save him either. How could she, when she couldn't even save herself?

But suddenly her fear evaporated. Faced with inevitable death, she now saw things differently: if she couldn't save any of them anyway, then she had nothing to lose. The wolf's paws became firm on the ground. Her panting slowed. Her hackles raised higher.

Snowfall knew what she must do.

They were trapped anyway, they were going to be killed anyway – she might as well fight. Maybe she'd surprise the human and get an advantage that way. Maybe she'd be able to save one of her pups.

And maybe not.

But she had only two choices: either fight and possibly die – or just die. So she would fight.

Clare leaned into the cave. It still looked empty. So far, so good. If the wolf pups were still here, they were hiding at the back.

She moved a few inches inside on unfeeling feet, and stopped again. Listened. She could hear her teeth chattering, but that was all. Smokey crowded behind her, touching her arm with his soaked nose. He wanted to get inside the shelter too.

"Sorry, Smokes," she said and stepped fully inside the cave. The gelding followed close on her heels, then moved past her toward the back part of the cave, his nostrils flaring. "Do you smell anything, buddy?" Clare said, her hand on his frigid shoulder.

The gelding snorted and raised his head, then spun so his heels were facing the pit at the back of the cave. Clare's heart began to hammer in her ears. Something *was* there!

But of course – the harmless wolf pups. If there were any adult wolves here, they'd know it by now. "It's okay," she murmured to the horse. "The mom and dad wolves aren't back yet, and as long as I can get a fire going, they won't come in. Everything's okay."

Smokey's eyes were so big that Clare could see the white rim glowing in the shadows. The horse kicked out with one back hoof, low, and the sound of his metal horseshoe scraping stone resonated through the cave.

Clare took a step back toward the cave opening. Maybe a big wolf *was* hiding deep inside. There had been that growl earlier, after all. She backed up a couple more steps. A wisp of wind touched her, the flakes riding it tickling her cheek and drifting on.

Smokey reared up, jerking the reins from Clare's grip. A scream like she'd never heard burst from his mouth and his hooves clattered on the stone as he frantically turned to face the back of the cave once again. Clare gasped and leapt back when he reared, his hooves striking out at the darkness.

Snow whispered against her hair, on her arms, on her face. A bit of wind touched her frozen pant leg. She had backed right out of the cave! She looked up to see spinning white, then turned in a complete circle to see white, white, white – and the dark gash of the cave opening once more.

Inside, the big gelding reared again but this time, the sound of his shoes scraping stone was oddly muted. It was as if the snow, that whispering death, was cocooning her, protecting her from the horrors that hid in the darkness within. Even Smokey seemed far removed, as if he were in another world.

Clare's arms dropped to her sides, too numb to hug herself against the cold any longer. But there was no need; she no longer felt cold. In fact, she wasn't even shivering now. Her teeth had stopped chattering.

But wasn't that a warning sign, a precursor to freezing to death?

She opened her eyes to see Smokey with his ears pinned

back, still staring deep within the cave. He needed her. She had to go back, if nothing else, to bring Smokey out with her.

But would he be any better off out here? Would he survive the snowstorm? Or was the unknown, hidden in the depths of the cave, the more dangerous of their choices?

In or out? Were there really no other options?

Smokey, my dear. I am here to help you. I am so glad that you called me and will do my best, but first, please allow me to lean on your side. My strength is gone. As I recover from my journey to this place, please tell me what I can do to assist you.

Ah, you and your girl have been caught in this storm. Your girl was unprepared for the freezing cold and so you brought her to this cave to shelter her — but when you arrived, a dangerous one waited, one who wishes you both harm.

Yes, I feel her too. Hatred emanates from her like heat from a fire. What a livid and violent emotion! You were right to call me. We must help her.

And your girl. Yes, your girl.

Clare thought again of moving forward, of attempting to get back barely inside the cave entrance, but her muscles didn't want to work. Lethargy had added itself to the numbness. And weakness. Her head felt like a huge weight on her shoulders.

She sank to her knees in the snow. She'd go inside… she would… in a minute. First, she'd rest here, gather her energy and strength, and then she'd move. She huddled down into a ball, even though she wasn't cold anymore – collapsing over her knees just took less energy than sitting upright. She turned her head sideways and stared out across the canyon, watched the snow fall, thick and heavy. Almost everything was white: the ground, the stones, the plants, the sky. Only the river burned a clear gray through the white, a long snake moving on in a world where everything else had disappeared.

Clare closed her eyes. Even though it took little energy to look, she could no longer bear to see the world vanishing around her. In this cold, even the river would soon be gone – covered by frost and ice. Once the ice took hold, the snow would have a place to land. The river, in a matter of hours, would become white too.

However, she would never see it, even if her eyes were open. She knew that now. She wasn't going to get up and walk back inside the cave. There was no help there anyway.

No way to get warm. Her body heat had dropped too low. Her world was ending too… She'd heard of how it felt to freeze to death. First, you got too cold and started to shiver, more and more violently until you suddenly stopped shivering. You stopped feeling the cold. That's when you drifted off to sleep, never to wake.

At least if she let it happen, Smokey should be okay. Without her to protect, he could run away. Without her to save from the wolves, he could save himself. He could probably survive the storm. He had a fur coat, and as long as he didn't get hurt in a battle with a wolf pack, he'd be able to find his way home after the wind abated.

It was a good reason to remain outside the cave. If she died inside, he might still try to protect her body. It was better to remain here, to live out her last moments peacefully, and in the process, save Smokey too. Not that she had a lot of choices. She couldn't move now anyway.

I'm sorry, Mom, she thought. I wish… But things weren't different. She had said those horrible things to her mom. She hadn't turned back when she'd been called.

There was nothing she could do but hope that her mom somehow knew that Clare loved her, fiercely and loyally, for there was no going back now – ever.

Snowfall had been looking for her opportunity to attack the large creature – her eyes locked on the long back legs as she searched for an opening to leap forward and rip the tendons – but then it turned toward her and struck out with its powerful front legs.

The light creature appeared out of nowhere. Snowfall jumped back as if bitten, and her lip curled as she glared at the creature. It looked like a human, but she knew it wasn't. It was something else altogether, something unique and powerful and pulsating with an energy that she'd never seen before.

Even more frightening, its energy became stronger as the seconds plodded past, until all Snowfall wanted to do was run and hide from the terrible strength of it. She backed up, step by slow step, to conceal herself behind one of the boulders. Something warm and soft touched her back legs and she glanced back to see Ice trembling as he looked up at her with terrified yellow eyes.

Snowfall glared back at the two malevolent creatures. Hate bloomed in her heart again. She had had enough. These creatures would terrorize her, her pups, and her brother no longer. She was going to do something to stop them – and she had to do it now! This strange new one was frightening, yes, but with every breath it grew stronger and more powerful. With every passing moment, her pups were in more danger. With every second, she lost a bit more of her advantage. The time to act was now, before it gained more strength.

Her hatred made her reckless and she stepped out from behind the boulder, standing tall and proud. Then, ignoring Ice's whine behind her, she stalked forward, emboldened by rage.

"You must come."

Clare heard the voice but didn't register what it was saying at first.

When the soft words repeated, she wondered if she were dead. Maybe angels were telling her to come into heaven. The voice certainly sounded angelic: gentle, loving, and even musical. Clare tried to move, but couldn't.

"I will help you stand. I will give you warmth."

A wonderful heat spread over her, like a blanket warm from the dryer but better – as if she were safe and special and cared for as well. She relaxed, sighing.

A thin, strong hand grabbed hers. "Please, stand. We must get inside the cave."

But I'm dead, thought Clare. There aren't any caves in heaven. She smiled. She'd never been to heaven before, so how would she know if there were caves or not?

The voice grew more insistent. "You must get up. Please, now. Hurry!"

What could be so urgent about heaven? Clare opened her eyes, then blinked. This wasn't what she expected. She was still outside the cave where she died, but Smokey and a strange girl were with her. And the snow was still falling. Clare shivered despite the warmth that engulfed her. What was she doing here? Maybe she wasn't dead. Maybe someone had simply come to rescue her.

"Who are you?" she asked.

"I am Angelica. Now please come with me, back inside the cave. It takes a great deal of energy to keep you warm out here."

"But…" Clare touched her own shoulder. There was no blanket draped around her. How was this girl warming her? She focused on the concerned face peering down at her. The girl, Angelica, appeared to be about seventeen years old, though she wasn't much taller than Clare. Her skin was pale, her hair a long, light blonde, and her eyes a striking gold color. "Weird."

Angelica laughed quietly. "Yes," she said. "But I prefer to be called *different*."

"Oh, sorry," said Clare and her hand went to her mouth. "I didn't mean… I just…"

"Please, come inside. We can talk in there, out of the storm."

Clare nodded and carefully rose to her feet. Her strength had returned? A miracle! Still she was cautious when she took her first step, not wanting to pitch headfirst into a snow bank. Smokey followed them as they made their way to the cave mouth.

"What are you doing way out here? And how are you making me warm?" Clare stopped and stared into the golden eyes. "I'm not dead, am I? Maybe it's a stupid question, but just in case…"

Angelica shook her head. "No, you are not dead, though I do not think you were far from death when Smokey called me here, just moments ago."

"Huh? What do you mean? How'd he call you? How does he even know you?"

Angelica ushered her deeper into the cave. "I will answer your questions inside. I am getting tired and cannot keep you warm for much longer without help."

"I don't understand."

"I know. Please, be patient."

Once inside the thick stone shelter, Angelica led Clare to the nearest cave wall and helped her sit down. Smokey clattered on past them and stared into the darkness at the back of the cave. Clare noticed he was standing with his ears pinned back and his nose jutting forward. His muscles were ridged with tension. Poor horse. But what could she do to calm him? Nothing. She focused her attention back on her strange companion.

"Who are you, really?" she asked, turning to where she thought Angelica was standing. The girl was gone.

And Clare was getting cold again already. What had the teenager done to make her feel so warm? Whatever it was, Clare wished she would've kept doing it.

She climbed to her feet, swung her arms, and jumped up and down – anything to stop the creeping cold. And as a bonus, maybe her crazy actions would give the residents at the back of the cave even more of a warning to stay back. The shelter was big enough for all of them, and as soon as they could, she, Smokey, and Angelica would leave the wolves alone in their den.

The teenager came back a minute later with her arms full of wood. She smiled at Clare. "You are feeling better?"

"I'm getting cold again."

Angelica lowered the wood to the floor. "It is good to exercise then, for a few minutes, while I light the fire." She

59

selected some small sticks and put them in a pile, then bent over them, her back to Clare.

"I'm so glad you have matches," said Clare. "Do you need to use my penknife?"

"No, I have all I need here." The girl smiled back at her. "What is your name?"

Clare had just opened her mouth to speak when Smokey's hooves clanged against rock. She spun toward him, her heart in her throat, just in time to see a large, almost white wolf dive for his back legs.

"No!" she screamed as Smokey struck out with a deadly hoof. And missed! The wolf snarled and clamped down on his leg, ripping at his tendons.

A sudden flash of light left Clare blind. "Smokey!" she yelled, blinking madly. What was the wolf doing to him now? She had to save him! She stumbled forward as her vision began to return, cringing when a silver streak shot past her.

The sound of Smokey's hooves stilled as she moved toward him. Clare blinked again to clear her vision. Her beloved horse was still standing. Maybe he was okay – for the moment anyway. There could be more wolves. She grabbed his reins. "Let's go, Smokey. Let's get out of here." She pulled him toward the brightness of the cave entrance.

The gelding followed her a few hesitant steps, then stopped. Clare shook with adrenaline and dread as she turned back to him. Maybe he *couldn't* walk anymore. Maybe the wolf had seriously hurt him.

"There is no need to leave. Only one wolf hates us and she is gone," Angelica said from behind Smokey.

Clare dropped the reins and hurried to where Angelica bent over the wound. Her sight had recovered enough from the bright flash to see details – but there weren't many details to see. The ragged wound was covered in blood. It oozed from the cut and ran down his leg in a thick, red stream.

Angelica's fingers touched the injury and she closed her eyes.

"Is he okay? Can you tell how bad it is?"

The older girl didn't look up. Instead, she wrapped her fingers tightly around the wound.

"And what was that light? Where did the wolf go?" Clare continued, panic rising in her voice. "Answer me."

"I will answer your questions, but first I think that Smokey needs some warmth." Angelica sounded exhausted. "Can you put some larger sticks on the fire before it goes out?"

Reluctantly, Clare turned away from her beloved horse to look at the small blaze. It had burned almost all of the small sticks around it and would go out in mere seconds if she didn't put on more fuel. "Don't you have more matches?"

"I have no matches. And I know how to treat Smokey's wound. Trust me." Angelica raised her head. In the light from the cave entrance, her eyes glowed gold.

Clare swallowed and took a quick step back. "Who are you? How did you find us here?"

"The fire first, please, then the questions." Though Angelica's words were polite, her tone broached no argument.

Clare scowled and hurried to the small flame. She picked up three small twigs and laid them carefully on top of the dying fire, then held her breath as she waited for it to flare up. Of course, Angelica was right. They needed the warmth and if they had no more matches, well, she had no choice but to obey. But she'd make the older girl answer her questions as soon as Smokey was okay and the fire was blazing away.

She looked back at Angelica. She was still leaning over Smokey's wound, her back to Clare, her long hair appearing lusterless and almost white. Hadn't it been a soft gold before? She needed to hurry with the fire, so she could see what Angelica was doing. Clare rooted through the pile of wood, selecting twigs that were the right size, breaking larger pieces in half, and putting them, gently, one by one, on top of the slowly growing blaze. Finally, the flames were licking through the sticks, catching and consuming them.

"Thank you, my friend."

Clare looked up. Angelica was standing at Smokey's head now. She frowned again when the older girl leaned forward to kiss Smokey on his lowered forehead.

Then Angelica turned to Clare. "There is no need to be afraid," she said in a soothing voice as she walked to the fire. Smokey walked behind her, not a trace of a limp in his step. "I am here to help and assist, not to do harm."

Clare hurried around behind Smokey and bent over the wound. It was gone. Puzzled, she looked at his other back leg. Maybe she'd been mistaken which... but no, his other back leg was unmarred as well.

Slowly she stood and watched the older girl place more

wood on the fire. Her hair was golden again, but that could just be the lighting. Smokey was healed, but his injury could have been a trick. Maybe Angelica had squirted some ketchup on his leg before Clare had looked at it, then wiped it away. However, there was no way to explain how the wolf had been chased off or deflected or *something* by a flash of light. That made no sense at all.

"Where did you come from?"

Angelica looked up at her from warming her hands at the fire. "That is hard to explain. I was not here and then I was here, because it was Smokey's wish that I come to help him."

"You realize that makes no sense."

Angelica shrugged. "Nevertheless, it is true."

"Okay, so let's say he can call for help," Clare said, sarcasm thick in her voice. She looked up at Smokey. He was watching Angelica with obvious adoration. Immediately, Clare felt ashamed. Though it made no sense, she couldn't shake the feeling that if Smokey knew she didn't believe Angelica, he would be disappointed in her. "So then, how does he know you? How do you know him?" she asked, forcing her voice to sound less resentful.

"Ah, Smokey and I have a history," Angelica said and turned her hands over. Her palms were spotless, as if they hadn't touched a wound or ketchup or anything else. "When he was a young horse, he called me," Angelica continued. "I came to him in time to find him trapped by a forest fire. I was able to help him that day, making the fire pass by and leaving him unscathed."

Clare stared at Angelica. "That was how he got his name. We named him Smokey because he came home smelling like smoke. And Mr. Davis said he must be charmed because no normal horse could've escaped from that fire. In fact, that's why he gave Smokey to me to train and ride, because he thought I would always be safe with him."

Angelica smiled. "I know. It was meant to be because you two were meant to be together."

Clare didn't know what to think – except that maybe Angelica wasn't *that* bad. If only her mom would realize the same thing about her and Smokey. She led the horse closer to the fire. They both needed to get warmer.

As she lowered herself to sit in front of the cheering blaze, Clare recapped the three things she knew about this girl. First, Angelica was extremely strange. Second, Clare didn't understand *yet* what was happening, but she would, despite Angelica's nonsensical, irritating responses to her questions.

But it was the third thing that troubled her most of all – today, this very unusual girl had saved both of their lives. Clare would have died out there in the snow. Smokey would have been injured, possibly fatally injured, if Angelica hadn't somehow repelled the wolf.

Without Angelica's help, they could both be wolf dinner right now.

Snowfall ran through the storm in a panic, loose snow
flying around her. That creature: what a horrible thing it
had been! Attacking her with a light force, the power of
which had flung her across the cave as if she was lighter
than air. As if she was nothing at all.

Was it chance that the creature had flung her
toward the exit to the den? Or was that part of its plan,
so her pups and brother would then be unprotected?
How she wished she'd turned back right then and
surprised the creature with a direct attack. If only she
hadn't rushed out into the storm without thinking, she
might have caught it unguarded, unaware. Once she
was outside, the creature had time to ready itself for
another attack. There was no way she'd get past it now
to save her pups and brother. They were alone now,
undefended.

She came to a halt when she reached her destination
– the top of a bluff that overlooked their den – and spun
around.

All she could see was white. Even the dark slash
of the cave opening wasn't visible through the heavy
snow. And up this high, the wind was harsh and cold.
She hunkered down and stared into the featureless
miasma. Somewhere in that direction, her pups were
unprotected. Her brother was dying. And it was all

because of humans – or creatures that looked human anyway. How she despised them!

What was that creature doing to her pups at this very moment? What terrible things?

And what was she going to do about it? How was she going to save them now?

What loathing haunts the silver wolf, what fear and despair. The poor, poor thing. She must be terrified for her pups now. And it is true that they need her – I can feel their trepidation as they cower at the back of the cave. They need to know she is here for them.

And she was so thin, like a fur-covered skeleton. I think she is starving.

I must go to her. I must find her and somehow explain to her that it is safe to return. She needs the shelter provided by her cave. She needs to return, knowing we will harm neither her nor her pups. She needs to rest here with them, reassuring them that all is well, that we are merely sharing their shelter while the storm lasts. Somehow, I must make her understand.

The fire's heat felt wonderful, though Clare's back was getting cold. She stood and faced away from the fire, looking out the cave entrance as she tried to organize her thoughts – what questions could she ask Angelica to get an answer that made some sense?

Unbelievably, the snow seemed to be falling even more thickly. It certainly was piling up faster and getting deeper with each passing minute.

"I must go," said Angelica behind her.

Clare turned to see Angelica pat Smokey's neck. "But what about the storm? You can't go out."

Angelica's forehead creased as she looked past Clare. "The snow is getting deep, but the temperature is no longer dropping and there is no wind in this canyon. I believe I will be safe."

"You should stay until it stops snowing at least. I need to go home too, but I know I shouldn't go right now. It's too dangerous."

"Thank you for being concerned about me…" Angelica paused. "I do not even know your name."

"Clare."

"Thank you for being concerned about me, Clare," Angelica repeated. "But I am not as vulnerable as you and Smokey in this storm. And unlike you, I am not thinking of going back to my home. In fact, I hope not to go far. It depends on the distance the wolf has traveled."

"The wolf? Why?"

"She is starving and needs help. She is weak and hungry. I must somehow communicate to her that we will not hurt her and that her cave is a safe place to be in this storm, even with us inside. Those at the back of the cave, her family, they need her too. She should know she is safe to return to them."

Clare couldn't stop herself from laughing with disbelief. Was Angelica for real? She already thought that horses could mysteriously call her and apparently she thought she could communicate with wolves too. "And how are you going to tell her that?"

"I do not know." Angelica frowned and her gaze wandered once again to the snow falling outside. "However, I must try."

"And what if she attacks you again?"

"I do not believe she will. She has no puppies to protect out there." Angelica glided toward the door. "I will be back soon." She walked into the storm and disappeared almost immediately.

Clare hurried after her, stepping into snow almost to her knees. She thought she saw a flash of gold to her left but wasn't sure. "Angelica?"

Nothing. Smokey nudged her back.

"Angelica!"

Silence. Clare turned to her horse. "I hope she's okay, Smokey. She's so freaky, but I still don't want anything bad to happen to her."

The gelding nickered and turned back into the cave. Clare searched the white expanse for a few more seconds, then shivered, wrapped her arms around her middle, and followed him back to the fire. She huddled close. What would she do if Angelica didn't come back? She looked up at the horse. "We'll go look for her if she's not back in an hour, Smokes. Even if it is cold." She looked down at the blaze. "We'll have to get some more wood anyway."

A scuffing sound reached her ears and she glanced back at the doorway. It was empty. But of course it would be. Angelica wouldn't be *that* quick.

So where had the noise come from? Her heart lurched when she realized that Smokey's attention was directed to the back of the cave. The puppies!

Clare stared past Smokey and a huge smile stretched her face. One of the wolf pups had come out of hiding and what a pretty thing it was! Almost white, and so fluffy and cute. Too thin, it was true, but not as thin as its mother. The grown wolf must be giving most of the food she caught to her pups.

She didn't see the two darker puppies behind the silver pup until one of them jumped on it. And to the right of them, another silver head peeked over the edge of the slope at her and Smokey, its yellow eyes like jewels as they caught the firelight.

Clare sat as still as she could as she watched them. The smaller she could make herself the better. Not that they'd hurt her; they were far too young for that, plus they didn't seem aggressive at all. However, if they came to investigate her, they might realize that she wasn't scary – and if that happened, they might think that *all* humans weren't scary, and there were lots of humans who'd shoot wolves who came too close.

Maybe I should frighten them back into the shadows, she thought as she reached out to touch Smokey's strong foreleg. But she didn't have the heart to do that. She'd feel so, well, *mean*. And besides, the pups had been cowering at the back of the cave for over an hour already. They must be getting bored.

She smothered a laugh when the medium gray pup pounced on the cautious silver one. She heard them roll to the bottom of the incline, sending a cascade of pebbles with them. The big silver one and the darkest one stopped mock fighting and cocked their heads as they waited for their siblings to join them again. They didn't have to wait for long. Moments later, the gray pup leapt over the bank, the small silver one right behind it. The four of them ran in circles, leaping and pouncing, panting and smiling, as if they didn't have a care in the world.

If only it were true – for all of them.

Her life force is so easy to follow. So bright, as if being hungry for too long has pared away all but the essential strength that remains at her core.

I wonder if she is watching me now?

Her trail leads upward, among the bluffs. Is she up there, looking down at me and wondering why I am following her? Or has she moved on?

I worry about communicating with her. Clare was right in her skepticism. Communicating with canines does not come naturally to me. Only if this wolf is very willing to hear what I have to say will she understand – and what if she does not want to listen?

But I am getting ahead of myself. First, I must find her. First, I must catch up to her. That, in itself, is a large enough task. That, in itself, I may not be able to accomplish.

Snowfall sensed the creature's approach before she saw or heard her. It was more an energy in the air that told her that the thing was drawing near than any of her senses. And somehow she could tell that the creature was looking for her. She slunk behind a boulder, keeping low, then peeked around the hard edge.

Yes, there it was. Now she could see it, struggling up the slope, almost as pale as the snow that made climbing the hill almost impossible, at least it had been that way for her – and yet this creature wasn't even breathing heavily. It didn't seem to notice the cold.

She retreated behind the boulder again when the creature looked in her direction. Had it seen her?

She couldn't take the chance that it had; she had to move on. She couldn't see the cave from here anyway, and now there wasn't as much need to do so. The creature was out here following her, so her pups only had the human to contend with. And Snowfall had been pleasantly surprised at how easily it had been affected by the cold and snow, at how weak it seemed. It may not even realize her pups were there. As long as the mischievous four remembered that even weak humans could be dangerous and stayed hidden, they should be okay.

But this thing, what was she to do with it? It was coming closer and there was no doubt in her mind now that it was hunting her. She had to do something soon, but what?

Kill it. Really, there were no other answers. She needed to get rid of it if she wanted to protect her pups, for it *would* go back to the cave once it tired of chasing her. It would find them there, helpless and unprotected – for in order to leave the cave, they would have to pass the human, and Snowfall was positive they would be too frightened for that. Even if they did muster the courage to leave the cave, maybe in a rush in order to catch it by surprise, they wouldn't get far. The snow was too deep for them.

So she would kill this thing, and then make her way back and rescue her pups. She'd kill the human too and chase the caribou-like creature away.

Snowfall turned her yellow eyes on her advancing predator. Now that she knew what to do, how was she going to do it? Last time it had thrown her aside as if she was nothing. It could do that again. A frontal attack was not wise with this one.

No, this time she must attack from behind and surprise it.

Snowfall slunk away from the thing. She had a plan: move along this ridge for a distance, then duck down on a side trail and hurry back below the creature. When she came up on the ridge again, she'd be behind it, and then she could surprise it, leap on it from behind before it had time to turn and fight.

She knew the perfect place too, not far off, with a hidden side trail. Soon, she and her family would be free of the creature and its dreaded human sidekick. And a bit of her thirst for revenge for the murder of her mate would be sated.

She was here behind this boulder just moments ago, but she must have seen me coming and left. I must hurry — I must catch her before she runs too far.

The snow is so deep now and the wind blows hard up on this ridge. It swirls the snow and makes it hard to see where I am going. The wolf has the advantage because she knows this land. It is her home. She could slip away so easily.

But wait. Her energy is no longer on the ridge top. She has gone down a side trail. Should I follow?

What's that? Oh my!

The wolf pups played for about ten minutes, leaping on each other and engaging in mock battles, then just like domestic puppies would do, they abruptly stopped.

Clare wasn't sure what to do as the large silver one cautiously approached her, its amber eyes locked on her own. She really didn't want to get too close to them. She'd never forgive herself if sharing the fire played a role in the puppies being unafraid of other people and then they were hurt. But she didn't want to leave the fire's warmth either.

Slowly, she backed away and the further she got, the more boldly the pup moved forward. Then the others followed their sibling. They settled down a few feet from the fire – not too close to be frightened by it, but close enough to feel some of its warmth – and flopped over each other in a multi-hued pile of fur. The last one to close her eyes was the silver female, but finally she too succumbed to her tiredness and her head lowered to rest on her brother's dark fur.

Clare shivered. It was cold away from the fire. The entrance to the cave was too big to keep the heat inside, even when she was closer to the back of the cave. And yet, she knew she shouldn't get closer to the pups. She wrapped her arms around herself and cuddled up to Smokey's shoulder and mane.

She glanced back into the shadows. Maybe heat had

collected at the very back of the cave, in the farthest corners from the door. It was unlikely, but she had to try. Anything was better than freezing or chasing the puppies away from the fire. They were obviously cold too or they wouldn't have crept toward the blaze to begin with.

She walked to the edge of the decline and started down the slope. "Just wait there, Smokey. I'll let you know if it's safe."

But the horse didn't want her to go alone. Carefully he stepped after her, skidded a bit on the slope, then steadied.

By the time they reached the bottom, Clare was glad he'd come along. It was so dark back here – and unfortunately, it was no warmer. She turned back to Smokey and stroked his warm neck. No matter how much she hated to do it, she was going to have to chase the puppies away from the fire.

"Let's go back, Smokes," she said.

But the horse was staring off into the darkest shadows, his ears at attention.

"What is it?" Clare whispered. "Is something—"

A growl interrupted her.

Clare froze. It was the same growl she'd heard before, the one she'd tried to convince herself was a puppy. But this was no puppy growl. It was the deep warning growl of an adult wolf. There was another wolf in the cave!

Snowfall watched the creature's tall thin form loom up before her as she stalked closer and closer. Its back was to her and it was walking away, totally unaware that death crept just a few yards behind it. Soon, she would be close enough to attack. Her eyes roamed over the silhouette. Would it be best to run forward and grab the creature by one of its slender legs, then pull back and unbalance it? Once it was down, she could go for its throat. Or should she leap upon its back and force it down that way?

The creature stopped suddenly. They'd reached the side trail that Snowfall had used to duck around behind the creature. But it *couldn't* know that Snowfall had gone that way. The wind and snow had obliterated her tracks and obscured the entire trail. So why did the creature pause?

Snowfall slunk slowly forward. Just two yards closer and she'd make her rush. She'd leap on its back, she decided.

One more yard.

The creature turned its head and stared straight at her. Their eyes met, blazing gold against burning amber.

How did it know she was there? How? She was sure she hadn't made a sound.

But however it sensed Snowfall, that didn't matter now. She lowered her head and growled. Tightened her muscles to spring forward.

A warm breeze brushed against her and she hesitated again. Warmth? Up here?

Then she felt it – a peacefulness sighing in her heart. For some reason, she thought of being safe in the cave, with her puppies beside her, content and happy. That was the way she'd felt when Avalanche was well, when Ranger was alive. It was how she felt when she was a pup herself, protected by her parents and the rest of her pack.

She lowered herself the rest of the way to the snow and stared at the creature. How could she feel this way when her enemy was right in front of her? Could the creature be…

Suddenly, it gasped and stared wildly about. The safe feeling evaporated, leaving an even bigger emptiness in Snowfall's heart.

So the feeling had been coming from the thing. It was a trick!

Fury engulfed Snowfall in a storm and she leapt to her feet, then surged toward the creature. A raging roar shot from her jaws. She would kill it. She would kill it now!

A flash of light caught her mid-stride and for a moment, she was blinded. She rushed ahead anyway, jaws snapping, trying to catch the creature's flesh between her teeth, ready to tear it to shreds.

But she ran too far.

Still halfway blinded, she spun around. The wind gusted uninterrupted past the spot where the creature had stood. The wolf shook her head. Blinked. Rubbed her eyes on her forelegs.

Yes, it really was gone. What was happening?

Clare pressed against Smokey's side. There'd been another wolf in the cave this whole time and none of them had had a clue, not even Angelica who supposedly knew how to talk to wolves.

"Back up, Smokes," she whispered to the gelding and tugged gently on his reins. Smokey took a slow step back, and another, and then they were at the base of the rise to the rest of the cave. All she had to do was lead him back up the slope – but if she turned him to climb away from the wolf, would it attack?

"Clare," Angelica's voice came from behind them.

Clare's shoulders sagged as relief flooded through her and she clutched at Smokey's mane. "Angelica, there's another wolf."

"I know." Angelica slid down to stand beside them. "I can see him in the darkness."

"Really? Where?"

"In that corner," she said, pointing. She glanced at Clare. "Can you keep Smokey here?"

Clare nodded. Like she *wanted* to get close to the wolf. But apparently, Angelica did. The girl bent low and crept soundlessly toward the wild creature. A soft hum, like distant wind, whispered through the cave. Clare tore her eyes from the dark corner to look up to the main chamber. Was the sound coming from there? Or outside?

Maybe the storm was entering the canyon. That would be just her luck.

Smokey drew her attention when he stepped forward. "No, Smokes," she whispered and tightened her grip on his reins. Then she saw why he was acting nervous. Angelica was almost to the wolf.

"You're getting too close." Clare's voice betrayed her panic.

"I believe he is injured."

"Injured wolves are dangerous, Angelica." Clare dropped the reins, commanded Smokey to stay, then hurried forward. The wolf pulled from the shadows as she moved closer. His lips lifted in snarl. Clare stopped short. "Don't get any closer, okay? He'll hurt you."

Angelica kept her eyes on the wolf as she spoke. "I do not think he will, Clare. He is frightened of me, that is all."

"But wild animals that are afraid are dangerous too. He might think he has to protect himself." Clare's eyes moved over the creature. He was dark, almost the same color as the shadow that held him. His eyes however, were a jewel-yellow, the same as the others. And he looked simply skin and bones, he was so thin. "I've heard that injured bears are the most dangerous bears of all. Maybe wolves are the same."

"Do not worry about me." Angelica sounded as if she was in a trance. That, or she was trying to lull Clare. "Please return to Smokey."

Reluctantly, Clare took a step back. "But, Angelica." Clare's voice grew louder as the older girl moved even closer to the wolf, her hand out. "Don't do that." She took a deep breath. The strange girl wasn't listening. "Angelica!"

The teenager ignored her and crept a few inches closer to the wild animal. At least it wasn't snarling now, Clare noticed with relief. Probably because she herself had stopped – it had only snarled when she'd come close, not Angelica. Maybe the girl did know some way to communicate with wolves. If only it were enough that he wouldn't attack.

As Angelica inched closer, the wolf tried to shuffle away from her but there was nothing behind him except a hard stone wall. And it was obvious now that the poor thing was seriously hurt. He moved by dragging or pushing himself with his front legs, rather than walking. Her eyes filled with tears. The poor thing. She was sure his injury would be fatal. No wonder he was starving. He'd need a lot of food to heal from such a devastating injury, if healing was even possible. The silver wolf might be able to catch enough to feed the puppies, but this dark wolf would need far more than she could ever hope to catch.

Smokey's hooves tapped against the rock as he moved closer to Clare. When he touched her shoulder, her hand went up automatically to stroke his face, but she couldn't look away from the drama unfolding before her.

Angelica stopped, crouched even lower, then slowly reached out. The wolf's gaze slipped from her face to her hand with white-eyed terror. He whined.

The wind murmur heightened again. Clare found herself relaxing as the song filled the cracks and crevices. It was so peaceful, so soothing, almost like a muted melody sung by a thousand angelic voices. And unbelievably, the wolf was relaxing too. His head drooped onto his front paws.

Clare held her breath as Angelica lowered her hand and touched his furred head. The wolf's eyes widened and he flinched, but he didn't try to move away.

"Clare, can you take Smokey into the front chamber of the cave now?"

More than anything, Clare didn't want to go. She had to see what happened. And if Angelica could ignore her when Clare advised her not to approach the wolf, then she could ignore Angelica.

"Clare?"

"I don't want to."

"Please?"

"No," she said with as much quiet firmness as she could muster.

"Then you must tell no one of what you see here today," said Angelica, turning to look at her. Clare gasped. Angelica's eyes blazed a luminous gold and she knew there was no way they could catch any light from cave entrance from down here. "Do you promise?" When Clare stood, speechless, Angelica repeated, "Do you promise?"

"I… I promise."

"Very well." Angelica turned back to the wolf, put her free hand on the wolf's backbone, and took a deep breath.

Her hands began to glow.

Clare stepped back and bumped into Smokey's shoulder. The horse nickered to her and then nuzzled her hand.

The glow moved up Angelica's forearms to her elbows, making her hands and arms appear translucent with light. The wolf whined and rolled his eyes in fear – but he didn't bite her. The light pulsed down into him, shone along his

spine for a moment, then lingered on his hindquarters before finally fading away – again and again and again. Angelica's head sunk lower as the light poured from her body to the wolf. Her hair grew dry and pale. Even her body seemed to become smaller. And yet she continued to pour *something* into the injured animal.

As the minutes ticked by, Smokey began to shift from side to side. When he nickered to Angelica, Clare felt the first twinge of fear. How much was too much? Was healing the wolf going to kill Angelica?

Smokey struck the stone with his shod hoof and the impact rang throughout the cave. The puppies started to yip – the noise must have awakened them. Then Smokey bobbed his head and struck again. His loud neigh slashed through the air.

The wolf looked up at him fearfully, but Angelica didn't move. The light pulsing into the wolf was much feebler now.

Finally, Clare sprang forward. Angelica was giving too much, she was certain of it. As she covered the last steps to the girl and wolf, the wolf jumped to his feet and staggered away on all four legs.

Clare knelt by the slumped-over girl. "Angelica, are you okay? Can you hear me?"

"I can." The words were so quiet that Clare barely heard her. "Is the wolf alright?"

Clare looked up to see nothing but shadow and Smokey approaching them. "He must be hiding behind one of the boulders. Or he left. I didn't see."

"He can walk." She sighed. "It was enough."
Unbelievably, she sounded satisfied, even happy.

"Are you okay?"

"Yes, I just need time. Either that or the assistance of Smokey, if he chooses to give."

Smokey sniffed at Angelica's head.

"What do you mean?"

"If he chooses, he can heal me."

"Like you healed him," Clare said, thinking aloud. "That's right, isn't it? You're magic. You healed him after the first wolf attacked him. That's why I didn't see a wound. And that's why your answers make no sense either. You're not normal. You're magic."

"It is not magic, but love. And tears given freely."

Clare frowned. "I gave my tears freely for my dad, but he still didn't come home," she said bitterly. "I gave my tears freely to my mom, but it's not going to stop her from ruining my life." She moved out of the way to let Smokey lean over Angelica. It was too dark to see his face so she reached out and ran her fingers lightly over his cheek. They came away wet. Immediately, she felt contrite about her outburst. "I didn't know horses could cry."

"I am so sorry to hear about your father, Clare," said Angelica.

Clare just shrugged. "It was a long time ago and I'm okay now." The last thing she wanted to do was talk about her dad. She felt depressed enough as it was.

"What did your mother do to make you cry?" Angelica sounded so compassionate.

"Actually, it was more than crying. I totally threw a fit," Clare admitted reluctantly. "But it was for a good reason. Mom said we're not coming back here next summer. That means that I have to leave Smokey, for good." Clare started to pace back and forth beside the horse. "It just makes me so mad, how someone can change your life like that, and I have no say over it at all. Mom doesn't know how much I love Smokey. She doesn't care that he means more to me than anything else."

Clare stopped abruptly when she realized that Angelica was staring at her. Her face burned and she bit her lip. "I didn't mean to tell you that," she said. "With everything else that's happened, the wolves and the storm and all, well, I guess Smokey and I might not seem that important. Not as life threatening anyway."

"It is important. This is your true wound, inside your heart. It cannot be masked by happenings." Angelica's eyes looked almost normal now, golden yellow and not doing that freaky glowing thing. The sympathy shining in them made Clare blink back tears as she lowered herself to sit beside the older girl.

"It terrifies me to lose Smokey too."

Angelica put a gentle hand on Clare's arm. "I only have one bit of advice. You must do what you believe right in all situations, even though your heart is torn."

Clare looked down at the ground. "But what good will that do? It won't stop Mom. And why should *I* have to sacrifice? I'm the kid. She's supposed to take care of me. She's supposed to *care*. I lost my dad. Isn't that enough?"

Angelica was silent for a long moment. "Your deep sorrow and confusion, even your anger, are understandable, Clare."

Clare nodded – but why did she feel that Angelica had left a big, fat *but* unsaid?

Angelica spoke again. "Do you know why she chooses to not return to your summer home?"

"Well, no," Clare admitted. "She started to tell me, but then I kind of blew up. I screamed horrible things at her." She drew a circle in the dust, then put an X through it.

"Maybe she made this decision because she feels it best."

"Yeah, but is it really the best just because she thinks it is? *I* don't think it's for the best."

"Then you must tell her that, in a calm voice, without anger and *with* understanding. It is the only way to get others to listen to you. Perhaps you should explain why Smokey is so important to you and that he provides you with great friendship."

Clare slashed her palm over the dust drawing, erasing it. "She knows all that, and she's still going to tear us apart. Can you do something? I mean, some magic, to convince her?"

Angelica sighed. "I am not magic, Clare, and for now, the only thing I can do is get you and Smokey safely home." Angelica rose gracefully to her feet, then held out her hand to help Clare up. "I will do my best to make sure that happens. However, I believe you can get through this. I believe you can do the rest."

Clare ignored Angelica's offered hand and climbed to her feet. "You don't understand anything. Mom has already made up her mind. She won't listen to anything I say." She grabbed Smokey's reins. "Come on, buddy. Let's get back to the fire."

After the creature disappeared, Snowfall wandered a complicated path, just in case it had somehow merely leapt out of sight and then hidden. After looping back on her own trail two times more, she was convinced it really had left. There would be no ambushing the thing.

Had it realized its danger and gone back to the cave to eliminate the weaker wolves first? Her heart wailed.

Snowfall leapt through the white powder – it was getting so deep that she could no longer run – panic rising in her like a whirlwind. Maybe it hadn't arrived back at the cave yet. Maybe it wasn't as fast as she was or didn't know the shortcuts. She could only hope.

Otherwise it could be hurting her puppies right now. It could be hurting poor Avalanche, unprotected and helpless at the back of the cave. Or it could be doing worse than merely hurting them! Fear, not the cold, made her body shake.

At long last, the cave mouth came into view. She stared down through the white flakes to see a bright light cast across the cave floor. What was it? It flickered like a forest fire, only smaller. The human was a horrible creature if it could create fire, possibly more dangerous than Snowfall had first suspected.

Were the three together again, inside the cave? She was sure she could take the big shaggy beast; attacking it once proved it was nothing more than a large caribou without horns. But the human? Obviously, its weak appearance belied its powers if it could command fire. And the other, the non-human... Snowfall whined. Was there anything she could do about that evil creature?

Clare held her hands out to the fire. "Are you sure we shouldn't chase them away?" she asked resentfully, looking down at the two puppies that were sleeping near her feet.

"There is no need to worry. I have communicated to them to trust only you and not other humans." Angelica flipped her blonde hair back from her face and stared out at the falling snow. "Look. The snow is lessening."

Clare jumped to her feet and hurried to the entrance. It was true, the flakes weren't falling as thickly and they were smaller. But even though the snow was decreasing, the day was growing dark.

"Dusk," said Angelica beside her, as if reading her thoughts. "Night is coming on."

Hot tears sprang to Clare's eyes. She couldn't stay out here all night. She just couldn't.

"All will be well," said Angelica and put a strong warm arm around her.

Clare's resentment immediately fired up again, and she pulled away. "How can you say that? There's no way you can know. Even if we get home safe, things are certainly *not* okay."

"You must have faith that all will be well, Clare. Sometimes it is just a matter of –"

"Well, it's a little hard to have faith when my mom is jerking me away from my home!" She was yelling, but she didn't care. "I lose my dad, *and* my home, *and* Smokey, and you say to have faith? How is faith going to change anything?" Clare stomped back to the fire, sending the puppies scurrying away. She felt completely miserable. Angelica didn't deserve her outburst and she knew it. But some things just *weren't* okay. Sometimes bad things *did* happen. Faith had nothing to do with it. She plopped down in front of Smokey and leaned back against his front legs. "You don't understand anything. Just leave me alone!"

"Clare." When only silence met her, Angelica sighed. "I will go get some more wood," she added, sounding contrite.

Clare didn't look up.

"I am sorry for hurting you, Clare."

Clare turned her head away. A few seconds later, she glanced back at the entrance. Angelica was gone. Immediately, she felt even worse. She was being so mean and here Angelica was just trying to make her feel better. And after she saved Clare's life and everything. She put her head in her hands. What a horrible person she was!

Smokey bent down and blew warm breath through her hair.

"What's wrong with me, Smokes?"

Again she felt his breath. Wrapping her arms tightly around herself, Clare lay down at his hooves and closed her eyes. She didn't want to think anymore. She didn't want to remember. She didn't want to face what a terrible person she was, how mean, how unkind… She didn't want to dwell on how many people she'd screeched at today. She just wanted to forget that this entire day had ever happened.

But more than anything, she wanted there to be no more pain, no more saying goodbye. She was so tired of goodbyes.

I do not know what else to do. Clare has her fire and soon will have more wood for it. She will survive the night. The storm is abating as well, so she will be able to ride home in the morning. The wolf at the back of the cave will not attack her. The pups will trust only her. So all seems well here – except she is so angry with me. I do not understand.

Neither do I understand the silver wolf's vehemence and hatred. She was on the ridge again for a time, but now is gone. Has she given up and abandoned her puppies? If so, I will have to help them. The other adult wolf is in no shape to support four growing puppies, though now he should be able to catch enough mice and small game for himself to fully heal. He will recover, but the puppies – they will not survive the harsh winter without their mother.

I feel so confused and helpless. So alone.

Clare was too cold to do more than doze for a long time, but then Angelica came back with more wood and stoked up the fire. As the pale girl moved around the cave feeding the fire and stacking the rest of the wood, Clare watched her through narrowed eyes. She didn't want Angelica to know she was awake. She couldn't face her own unkindness to the girl, not yet. There would be time in the morning to say she was sorry.

When Angelica went out again, Clare guessed she was going to get more firewood, enough to last for the entire night. She relaxed in the new warmth from the healthy blaze, and heard the scrape of iron shoes on stone as Smokey lay down behind her. When he was settled, Clare closed the distance between them, pushed her back up against Smokey's warmth, then closed her eyes and slept.

The night is half gone. Clare is sleeping soundly. It is nice to see the lines of worry, fear, and anger gone from her face. At least when she sleeps, she is at peace.

Smokey loves her so. He has lain there beside her for hours, keeping her back warm, even though I know it is not comfortable for him. He is a good and true friend to her. Clare is right – he will miss her terribly when they are separated.

And yet what I say is right too. Clare needs to have faith. And she needs to remember that she was not the only one who lost someone – her mother too lost someone very precious to her when Clare's father died. She and her mother need to pull together in times of strife, not farther apart.

Skýfaxa? Yes, I hear you. Yes, I can come right now. Soon I will be at your side.

Snowfall stared out at the open tundra, her eyes narrowed against the wind. Though the snow was lessening, the storm itself showed no signs of abating. A particularly strong gust of wind blasted her and she crouched lower to the ground. She *could* keep going. The wind wasn't able to stop her, not if she really wanted to leave the canyon, though the going would be difficult.

And there was no reason to stay now. When she'd finally realized that the powerful creature had arrived back at the cave before her, she knew with a dreadful certainty there was no hope left. Her puppies, her dear puppies, didn't stand a chance, and neither did Avalanche. Even if her family had survived an onslaught from the human, they would never survive the powerful non-human.

Yet that same impulse that had driven her away from the den where her family had been murdered wouldn't let her run too far from their lifeless bodies. She would go no farther tonight.

Snowfall sat on her haunches and threw her head back. A long mournful howl burst from her open jaws and added strength to the shriek of the wind. She'd failed them all, every one of them. They'd died despite her best efforts, and now there was nothing to do but cry.

*Skýfaxa, my cloud-maned one, here am I. What do you need, my beauty?*

*Oh my, your foal has been taken from you in a horse trailer. My dear, I understand your fear. I understand that it was too soon to let him go.*

*Let me go to where he is. Let me speak with him.*

*Skýfaxa, do not worry. I will return shortly.*

She was riding Smokey across the tundra at a full gallop. His muscles moved them forward at an unbelievable speed, and his stride was longer and more powerful than ever before. Arctic birds flashed and darted, wheeled and rejoiced in the air alongside them. Then she noticed the wolves and laughed for joy – four sleek adult wolves easily kept pace beside them, two silver, one almost black, and one in between: the puppies, all grown up. Their tongues lolled from their grinning mouths and their eyes exuded their pleasure as they raced alongside her and Smokey.

Something touched her back and in her dream she turned to see nothing behind her. Wait. It wasn't nothing anymore; something was growing in the air. A darkness. She turned away from it and leaned over Smokey's back. "Faster, boy, faster!" she yelled. And he ran faster!

But they couldn't run fast enough to leave the thing behind. She felt it move again against her back. Her dream wavered, grew thin, then began to shift into nothingness. She tried to pull it close, tried to save it, but then she was waking up.

"No," she murmured, and speaking chased the dream even farther away. She felt the warmth of Smokey's body leave her and heard the ring of his hooves on stone as he stood. His movement had been the touch that had forced her back to miserable reality. She opened her eyes.

The wolf puppies were curled up around her – one under her neck, two next to her stomach. She couldn't see behind her bent knees without disturbing the dark pup by her neck, but she was sure the fourth was sleeping there. She could feel its warmth soaking into her legs like a little hot water bottle. She reached out cautious fingers and stroked the puppy nearest her hand. The small wolf looked up at her with sleepy eyes, then slowly climbed to its paws, leisurely stretched and yawned, then leapt on the dark puppy that shared the spot next to Clare's stomach. The dark pup awoke with a yip and the two of them rolled into a tussle. Clare giggled and the pup by her neck looked at her, took a swipe at her chin with its tongue, then joined the fray. The pup at her knees was next, leaving Clare with four cold spots where they'd snuggled next to her. She sat up, smiling at their antics. They were so cute, so completely adorable.

"Good morning, Smokey. Thanks for keeping me warm last night." She stretched, stood, and gave the horse his morning hug. "I wish I had some food for you but we'll both have to wait until we get home." Her stomach rumbled loudly as if it was telling her to hurry.

Clare walked to the entrance to the cave. Mornings came early in the north, far earlier than in the southern reaches, and this morning looked glorious. The sun was shining and even though snow still covered the ground, it was obviously melting. The day was already getting warm. Freak snow storms could happen any time of the year up here, but there was one good thing about them – the snow usually didn't hang around long afterward when it was still summer, even late summer like now.

The snow stretched away from them, unbroken and unmarked. Worry darkened Clare's mind and she looked back into the cave. "Angelica? Are you here?" There was no response. "Angelica?" she called again even louder, but still nothing.

Clare turned back to face the sunny day and cupped her hands around her mouth. "Angelica! Angelica!" she yelled, then paused, listening. The only sound was birdsong from the willows lining the river below. If she really strained, she could hear the sound of the rushing river, but no answering voice.

She turned to Smokey. "We should get going, boy. We'll look for her on our way and if we can't find her, we'll get help as soon as we get home." She patted the gelding on the shoulder, then stepped out into the snow. She grimaced as she scooped up a large armful of wet mush and hurried it back to the fire. It was almost out anyway and there was no wood nearby for it to ignite, but since she wasn't going to be here to keep the puppies from getting too close, she wanted it extinguished. The ashes sizzled as the fire died. Smoke billowed upward. Clare moved, coughing, to the back of the cave and looked around for the puppies. They were nowhere to be seen.

"Good-bye, puppies. I wish you the best. I hope your mom comes back soon."

A flurry of movement from the shadows sent her stepping back in alarm. After all, the other adult wolf was still back there and Angelica had healed him – he was bound to be hungry. She exhaled in relief as the puppies raced toward her.

"I'll miss you guys," she said, as she bent to pet them. "You're so awesome. And just remember, some people aren't as nice as I am, so be careful."

She hurried to Smokey's side and led him from the cave. As soon as they were clear of the low ceiling, she jumped aboard. She turned back to the cave opening before getting the gelding to start for home. Sure enough, all four pups were sitting at the snow line and watching her. "Bye, guys." Even though she knew it was silly, she waved. Then she asked Smokey to walk on.

The snow was past his knees and he tested each step before trusting the rocks beneath the soggy whiteness as they started down the trail. Clare looked up the slope and down, as they advanced, but there was no sign of Angelica.

Maybe she got lost when she went out to collect firewood. Or maybe she'd gone after the mother wolf again. A shiver jittered down Clare's back, then disappeared. No, she could guess where Angelica had really gone – she'd returned to her home and didn't wake Clare before she left to say goodbye.

Shame colored Clare's face. She didn't blame Angelica. It wasn't as if she'd been very nice to the older girl, and after Angelica had saved her and everything. She looked down at the top of Smokey's head. He'd be ashamed of her too if he understood how mean she'd been to Angelica.

Smokey stopped and snorted, then looked back the way they'd come. Clare's gaze followed his. "Oh no," she whispered.

The puppies lunged through the snow behind them, leaping from one of Smokey's tracks to the next. The big silver pup stopped when it neared Smokey's hindquarters, looked up at Clare and barked, a happy grin on its innocent face.

Clare frowned at it. She had to get them back to their den. The puppies had no idea of the awful things that could happen to them, alone and unprotected, in the big wide world. She couldn't just abandon them out here, yet she couldn't take them home with her either. They'd be safe from predators then, but that was all. At best, they'd be sent to a zoo or wildlife sanctuary. They wouldn't be wild wolves anymore.

Returning them to the cave had to be the right thing to do. Surely, their mother would come back to care for them as soon as Clare left.

But how was she going to get them to turn back?

*Máni, it is I, Angelica. Your dam, Skýfaxa, asked me to come to you. She is so worried for you. She thinks you have been taken from her too soon.*

*And you say you want to leave this place. You miss your dam. You miss your own pasture, your own home. Here you are alone in this big stall, and though you can hear the horses on either side of the partitions, you cannot see them. You ache for company, for companionship. And being in a stall is not the same as running beneath the moon you were named for. It is not like living in the pastures, where you gallop through sun-drenched fields at your dam's side.*

*Come, I will take you home. We can only hope the humans here will understand.*

*Ah, yes, it feels good to be back outside. The night sky stretches over us like thick black ink. The stars are brilliant, like a billion burning diamonds. And there, over that low hill, the moon sets.*

*Come Máni, we must not linger. Dawn is quickly coming on and we have far to go.*

*Why do you pause?*

*I hear it now too. A door opening softly – the sound comes from the house. Strange, for the windows are dark. All inside should be asleep.*

*So who is this, slipping around the side of the house?*

Snowfall opened her eyes to white. Nothing but white. Then she raised her head and shook it, and snow went flying. The world reappeared.

Weakly, she climbed to her paws and looked about. The storm had stopped. The snow was quickly melting. The time had come to choose. She must go one direction or the other, back or forward. Back to investigate the bodies of her dead puppies or forward to escape the human and the creature?

Her legs were weak with indecision. She couldn't bear leaving her puppies, even their lifeless bodies, and yet she wanted to live herself.

And there were no other choices, no other options. She had to do one or the other. Forward or back.

"Go home, puppies!" Clare yelled in her meanest voice.

The medium gray pup cocked its head to the right and the dark pup to the left. They looked so cute that Clare almost laughed – almost. The situation was too serious for that.

She didn't dare try to turn Smokey on the dangerous slope, so she slipped from his back and walked toward the puppies waving her arms. If she could scare them back into the cave, all would be well. She scooped up some snow, shaped a snowball, and threw it so it landed in front of them. The dark pup leapt on the spot where the snowball disappeared and plunged his nose into the snow. When he looked up at her, his face was white. Clare couldn't help it – she laughed.

The little wolves leapt toward her, playful yips coming from their grinning mouths. Clare put her hands on her hips as she watched them bound the last few feet. "What am I going to do with you? Angelica shouldn't have told you that I'm not scary."

When the puppies reached her, they jumped around her, joyous to be on an outing. They must be so tired of staying in the cave, Clare thought. She bent to pet them, then looked up the hill at the cave entrance again.

The opening was dark as pitch. Clare shivered. There was no sign of the wounded adult wolf. She probably could return the puppies safely. But really, she didn't want to go back in there. The other wolf hadn't shown any friendliness at all. He hadn't shown any animosity either, but that was after Angelica had communicated to him that they were only going to be there overnight. If she walked back into the cave, into the shadows – well, who knew what he would do if she violated his home a second time. And there was no way she could make the pups stay in there anyway, once she had them back inside.

"Come on, puppies," she said, and turned back to Smokey. If she couldn't make them return to the cave and couldn't take them with her, there were only two options left – either find their mother and return them to her, or find Angelica and hope she could communicate to them to return to the cave. The problem was that she had no idea where to find either. Of the two though, she infinitely preferred to find Angelica, not only because she was by far the least dangerous, but because Clare knew that she really should apologize as well.

She scowled. It was just that comment Angelica made – as if anyone could change things just by having faith that things were different. And then when she'd said that Clare should talk to her mom calmly, as if she thought she knew all about Clare's mom.

She stomped the last few steps to Smokey, the wolf pups close on her heels. Her irritation was returning and she didn't want it to. Angelica had a right to say what she thought without Clare being rude to her – she had to remember that and control her anger. And she really wasn't angry at Angelica anyway. She was mad at her mom and didn't *want* to speak to her calmly. Poor Angelica was just the only person around for her to yell at.

A boy slips through the shadows to the stables, a boy with a soft step and cat-like movements. And though it is still dark, I can sense that he is troubled.

You know this boy, Máni? You say he was here to meet you this afternoon when you arrived. His face lit up with guarded joy as he touched your nose, stroked your dark mane. He wanted to promise you many things and you could feel his sincerity. He wants to always care for you; he wants to always love you; he wants to always be your friend.

You want to go to him, my dear? To say goodbye before you go?

And you want me to come. Yes, I will accompany you.

Snowfall came across the scent moments after the den came into view. The puppies and Avalanche had come this way. They were alive! Avalanche was finally well enough to walk; she could see his tracks in the snow. Relief and hope bloomed in her heart.

And confusion.

Why were they were tracking the dreaded human? It made no sense for Avalanche, even if he were now well, to allow the pups to accompany him on such a dangerous hunt.

Snowfall peered off in the direction that the tracks led. They were heading toward the river. Keeping low, she crept along their trail. She didn't understand what was happening, why they were following the human, but she was overjoyed that they were alive.

Now all she had to do was rescue them, and this time she wouldn't fail them. This time she would prevail.

He is so frightened of me. See how he has jumped back. Tears are in his eyes, though I do not think that is because I have frightened him. I think he is sad because he thought you were gone.

Please, Máni, approach him. Let him know you are his friend. He needs you.

See? He is not so scared with you by his side. Hold there, while I talk to him. Let him hug you.

The boy is sad because you were meant for his older sister and not for him. He will not be allowed a horse for two more years, and by then, you will not only belong to his sister, but he is sure you will love her as well. He says he came from the house while the others were sleeping to spend time with you, so you will love him too, even a little.

And more — he feels in his heart that he is your boy.

You feel as if he is your boy too? But what about the girl that you are meant for?

Wait, I have an idea.

Clare felt unnerved when she first saw the river – it was much higher than it had been the day before. The sound of the water was different from the happy, bubbly noise she'd heard early yesterday and much changed from the muted, misty sound she'd heard later, floating through the thick snowfall. The river was neither bubbly nor smothered in snow now. Instead, it rushed past, a murky current crowding the snow covered banks, as if it were in a hurry to escape the canyon. She could even hear deep, intermittent rumbles as the water's force pushed loose boulders over the immovable stones on the river's bed.

She shook her head. Why was she looking at things so negatively? The rising water was good news in a way. It meant that the snow was quickly melting in the morning warmth. No wonder she was only slightly chilled.

She glanced back at the puppies. "Come this way, guys," she called as she reined Smokey into the willows. It would be slower going through the brush than on the trail beside the river, but at least the puppies wouldn't get too close to the current. If one of them fell in, they wouldn't stand a chance unless she dove in after them to help them to shore – and she really didn't want to do that. It wasn't the depth of the water that scared her, or the strength of the current. She thought she could handle both of those, though they would be a challenge. But the freezing cold of the snow

113

run-off would be excruciatingly painful and dangerous. She could possibly even get hypothermia. And of course, the poor puppy with its small body mass and thinness would be even worse off.

She looked back. The puppies were right on Smokey's heels as if they were afraid to get too far away, now that they were a distance from the cave. It was as if they knew they were at risk out here in the big wild world.

Clare inhaled sharply. What was that dark shadow in the willows?

"Whoa, Smokes," she murmured and the horse stopped.

The puppies stopped too, then looked up at her with worried faces. They sensed her concern. Smokey did as well. He spun around to face the puppies and the river without Clare directing him. They all stood silent, waiting. For what? The mother wolf? A grizzly looking for fish?

A dark wolf limped into view beside the river.

The wounded wolf. So it *was* following them. The wolf froze when he saw that they'd seen him, his pale gold eyes staring at them unblinking. A low growl rumbled toward them, and Smokey shifted nervously beneath Clare. She laid her hand on his shoulder to calm him.

Then, like a mirage, another wolf appeared beside the dark wolf, glowing silver in the sunlight. She yipped once and the puppies rushed toward her en masse.

Clare smiled. The puppies were reunited with their mother. What a relief! She almost laughed aloud when the big silver pup made a flying leap for her mother's nose, tongue already out, ready to lick her. The others swarmed

around her front legs, yipping joyously. The dark pup chased the smaller silver one for a few feet through the snow, then the silver turned and, with a big grin on its face, met the dark pup head on. The mother wolf started jumping around, making short bursting runs to and from her puppies as she got into the spirit of things. Even the dark wolf seemed to forget Clare and Smokey were watching as he sat and enjoyed the celebrations, his tongue lolling from his mouth.

Clare tightened the reins and Smokey backed a step. The silver wolf caught the movement and stopped short, glared at them. Her clear eyes stared into Clare's, then her lips pulled back and she growled. Her hackles rose.

"It's okay, mama wolf," Clare murmured as she backed Smokey farther away. "I'm not going to hurt your babies."

The wolf lowered her head and the growl grew louder. The other adult wolf was growling again too now.

The medium gray pup rushed to its mother's forepaws, but she nipped at it, sending it scurrying back to its littermates. Then she stalked toward Clare and Smokey, rage blazing in her eyes like a golden flame, the dark wolf right beside her.

Here we are, Skýfaxa. We have arrived at the place where your son awaits. Thank you for trusting my light to bring us here. And thank you for your healing tears.

Máni and his girl are in the stable yard while the boy looks on. You know what to do.

Skýfaxa tolts toward them, her flaxen mane and tail flying. She neighs in greeting.

They all turn to look at her.

And now the most important step – she needs to approach the girl and not just Máni, her beloved weanling. She needs to see if this is "her" girl.

Oh my. The girl lets Máni's lead rope grow slack. She is overcome by Skýfaxa's magnificence. I can see tears in her eyes as she watches this beauty tolt toward her.

Skýfaxa stops, just two yards from the girl. Nickers gently. The girl steps forward and touches her starred face reverently. Skýfaxa nuzzles her, then when Máni approaches, she nuzzles him. Then the girl again. She adores this girl already and the girl seems totally and completely in love.

The girl calls for her mother in a breathless voice. Please, please, may this plan work!

The human looked frozen sitting there on the large caribou-creature, staring down at her with eyes the color of the sky. It didn't try to defend itself, didn't run or try to hide – it just looked at her, terrified.

Good. It would be easier to kill if it was frightened. It would panic and not fight as well. Snowfall's gaze lowered to the creature the human sat upon. There was fear there too, but more as well. There was fight. The caribou-creature wouldn't be as easy this time.

She heard a scuffle in the snow behind her but didn't look back. She'd told her pups to stay. They wouldn't go against her orders.

A tiny yip proved her wrong. Ice was at her paws, looking up at her imploringly. Then Aurora joined him, and finally Scout and Tundra. She couldn't effectively attack the creature with the puppies right there.

She looked up to see that the caribou-creature had backed even farther away from her – but when she tried to follow, Aurora blocked her path. Tundra pulled on her tail. Ice and Scout barked.

Snowfall stopped and stared at the human with narrowed eyes, then lowered her head to nuzzle Aurora. Maybe they were right. Maybe it was too dangerous. If she were kicked or injured by the big caribou-creature, she wouldn't be able to hunt and they'd be in the same situation they were before. Maybe it would be best to let the human and its creature leave – for that was obviously what they wanted to do – and save the fight for another day. Besides, this human was just a pup. Maybe they didn't become cruel and murderous until they grew up.

She turned and trotted away from the two creatures, the puppies running at her heels in a silvery jumble. Avalanche quickly joined her and trotted at her side. Now that the decision was made on postponing her revenge, it was time to leave this canyon. They needed to get out on the tundra and hunt some large game. Avalanche was well enough to help her catch enough to feed the pups and themselves. Then at last she'd satisfy her puppies' gnawing hunger. At last she could feed herself. A blissful mood settled over her as she trotted beside the river. Their ordeal was over. They had survived.

All is well. The mother and father have given their permission. Skýfaxa and Máni both have their own special humans: The sister, Cara, belongs to Skýfaxa, and the boy, Hans, to Máni. His tears have been replaced by a huge smile and laughing eyes.

Now they just have to get permission from Skýfaxa's people, which she is sure they will give. They have been spending less and less time with her as their lives have become busier. Even when Máni was born, they did not have time to teach him the things he needs to know to be a horse companion to humans.

Most interesting of all, Skýfaxa and Máni are together again. Not reunited at their previous home, but with this new vibrant family, who adore them already.

Sometimes it is so wondrous being a guardian of horses. I wish it could always turn out so perfectly!

Clare breathed a massive sigh of relief when the silver wolf turned away from her. She'd never seen such intense hatred in a glare before. For some reason, the mother wolf hated them both, though her rage seemed more directed at Clare. The girl had felt the wolf's loathing like a living thing brushing against her skin. Locked in that malignant gaze, she'd felt frozen and terrified, and even worse, she hadn't been able to think clearly at all. If Smokey hadn't been so steady and calm, she probably would have slipped from his back and run away – and that would have been the worse thing she could have done. At least on Smokey's back, she had some protection and speed, though how much protection was in question. Pure hate was a powerful motivator and if the wolf was motivated to kill… A wave of nausea hit her.

But it didn't happen, thought Clare. She didn't attack us, thanks to the puppies.

If the puppies hadn't rushed to their mother when they did, she was positive that the wolf would have struck – and the dark wolf too because he was obviously following her lead. In the face of the mother wolf's rage, the fact that Smokey towered over them was insignificant.

The puppies had saved them.

"Let's get out of here, Smokes." Clare's hands shook as she turned the gelding.

A large splash came from behind them, followed by a chorus of barks and howls. What was happening? Clare spun Smokey around again, just in time to see the female wolf sweep past on the current, her paws thrashing the water as she struggled to reach the shore. Somehow, she'd fallen into the rising river!

Clare galloped Smokey back to the riverbank – just in time to see the dark puppy float past, his head barely above the water. He was trying gallantly to swim to shore, but his efforts made no difference. The current was too strong. Clare saw a third head above the water, a small silver one, closer to the shore. The snow bank had given away, throwing the three into the river. The silver pup was caught in a whirlpool, swirling around and around, alternately yipping and choking.

The last two puppies milled about on the bank, obviously not knowing what to do, while the dark adult wolf followed the two who were floating downstream. He stopped short when he saw Clare and Smokey, looked after the disappearing heads with despairing eyes, then threw back his head and howled. The haunting sound sent a chill down Clare's back, but didn't stop her from directing Smokey to the bank.

"Go, Smokes! Go!" The horse paused at the edge, stared over the rushing current, and a high, rolling snort burst from his nostrils. "Hurry, buddy," Clare added and clamped her legs against his side in preparation.

He leapt off the bank and landed in water up to his belly. The splash instantly soaked Clare's legs and sprayed the rest of her body. The shock of the freezing cold droplets made her want to scream and her feet were already burning – which meant the puppies didn't have much time. She directed Smokey after the dark puppy first. At least, the silver one was going in circles. It would still be there after Clare had rescued the dark one, as long as she was fast enough. At this temperature, the pups would only last a few minutes. Soon they'd be too numb to struggle and the current would pull them down.

She and Smokey splashed through the water toward the dark pup. He looked like he was failing already. His little nose was barely above the water now and his paws made feeble splashes as his muscles became unresponsive. Slowly, slowly, they gained on him. First, he was at Smokey's nose, then his shoulder. Clare leaned down, one hand clutching Smokey's long mane with all her strength and grabbed just as the puppy went under. And missed!

In a last effort, Clare plunged her hand into the water where the puppy had disappeared and closed her fist. She was sure she had something in her grip, though her hand was too numb now to tell for sure. She did! A puppy tail!

The puppy was too cold to even yip in pain as she pulled him from the water – but he was still alive and that was what mattered. He blinked at her with a stunned expression as she hauled him onto Smokey's back. The gelding turned toward shore of his own accord as Clare searched wildly for the second puppy. It was the strongest, fattest pup of the bunch, so it would last longer than the puppy she held in her arms. It could still be alive, caught in the back eddy.

It was! She could see its silver head above the dark water.

"H…hurry, S…S…Smokes," she chattered and picked up the reins.

She directed him near the bank then pulled him to a quick halt, took the dark pup in both hands and tossed him onto a snow bank beside the river. The poor pup lay there – but she didn't have time to stop and help him now. His sibling needed rescuing too.

Smokey moved quickly toward the second pup and as they approached, Clare watched the cycle of the back eddy that the pup was caught in.

There! That was the place to stand and wait for the pup to brush past them. She halted Smokey at the right spot and waited as the puppy was swept toward them. It was a fast eddy, whipping the puppy and flotsam around in an endless circle. She leaned out… And caught the puppy by the scruff of its neck. She had it!

With the second puppy safe in her arms, Clare turned Smokey toward the bank. The gelding picked his way through the rocks with more care, now that they weren't in a hurry, and not for the first time, Clare marveled at what a wonderful horse he was. Not many horses would leap into a raging river. Not many would hurry through the current – most would pick their way along like he was doing now, even when it was an emergency, *if* they entered the river at all. And earlier, he'd saved her from the wolf's attack, and he'd called Angelica to save her from the storm. What was she going to do without him?

"Clare!"

Angelica was on the bank, holding the dark pup. "You

must hurry. Bring the puppy to me. The mother wolf needs you too. She will not last long."

Clare's gaze followed Angelica's pointing finger as Smokey pushed the last yards through the current. At first she didn't see the silver wolf fighting to keep her head above the water. The froth from the river where it was sucked beneath the logjam almost hid her. But then she caught sight of the pale head where the mother wolf was being pushed against the logs so hard that she couldn't swim away. A dreadful certainty settled around Clare. Once the mother wolf was too tired to keep her head above water, the current would pull her beneath the pile of logs and she would drown.

"But I can't …"

"You can. I know you can. I have faith in you." Angelica stepped forward to meet her as Smokey clambered out of the river. His entire body was trembling in the cold. Angelica quickly slipped the bridle from his head and laid it across his withers. Then she took the second puppy from Clare's arms and nodded toward Smokey's mechanical hackamore bridle. "You can use that to pull her out."

"C…can't you help?" Clare said, picking up the leather in shaking hands.

"I will come as soon as I can, but I must first warm these little ones or they will die."

Clare believed her. Both of the puppies bundled in Angelica's arms were barely moving. They needed attention at once.

"Be careful, Clare."

Clare nodded and looked toward the wolf again. She was still there, but her struggles were becoming weaker. She slid from Smokey's back. "Stay here, Smokes. Let Angelica warm you too." Then she hurried toward the logjam on numb feet.

Snowfall tried clambering up on the log in front of her again, but just as the two times before, her forelegs weren't strong enough to pull her own mass from the clutches of the river. The only difference was that this time she slipped more quickly, fell sooner, and then splashed back into the water to be pulled beneath the surface. She struggled to swim against the current drawing her deeper beneath the logs, but it was so hard. Her muscles were hardly working anymore because she was so cold, and she felt so tired, so weak. Maybe she should just give up and let the current have her.

But then the image of Aurora swirling in the current, around and around, swept into her mind. Scout, her smallest pup, was being carried toward the logjam and would be there any second. He didn't have the strength she did and would be sucked beneath the water to his death almost immediately. She had to grab him before that happened.

With a supreme effort, Snowfall fought her way to the surface and gasped for air. Then she looked for Scout. He was still nowhere to be seen – which made no sense. The snow bank had given way, throwing them into the river in the same place and at the same time. The same current was carrying them both, even though it carried her a bit faster because she was bigger and her body went deeper in the water. But not that much faster. He should have reached the logjam by now.

Unless she'd missed him and he was already down there. Already dead.

If she hadn't been choking for air, she would have broken into a mournful howl. She'd missed her baby. She hadn't been able to save him.

She noticed movement along the bank as if through a fog – then suddenly, when she realized what she was staring at, her vision cleared. The human was running toward the logjam. Running toward *her*.

Would these trials never end?

Clare stopped when she reached the logjam. Her gaze traveled over the heap of logs, branches, and other woody debris. If she climbed out onto that small log, while holding that branch, then she might be able to climb down onto the bigger log, the one that ended near the wolf. She'd have to lean over the end of it, but it should be safe enough, as long as her weight didn't make anything shift. That would be disastrous. If she fell in, she'd be in the same deadly situation as the wolf, fighting to stay alive in the frigid water with a current trying to drag her down to the depths.

Don't think about that, she commanded herself and hung the hackamore over her shoulder as her mom did with her purse. She wasn't sure what she was supposed to do with it. Angelica said to use it to pull the wolf out, but how? Put it around the wolf's neck?

She stepped on a bendy branch sticking out of the logjam, then pulled herself up onto the smaller log, clutching the branch she'd decided to use for balance. Carefully, she inched along its length. She had to move slowly because the log was narrow, slippery, and still covered with snow. Her grip was weak because of the cold. Thank goodness the snow had melted or fallen from most of the smaller branches.

She reached the end of the smaller log and lowered to sit

on the snow, then slid down to the larger log just above the surface of the frothing torrent, her eyes searching.

The wolf stared at Clare with a gaze bright with terror and rage. Clare clutched at the log. How was she going to approach this wild animal? The wolf hated and feared her and would harm her if she could. Just one snap from those powerful jaws could throw Clare off balance and into the current. Then they'd be struggling for their lives together, side-by-side – a struggle neither of them could win.

"It's okay, wolfie," Clare murmured, just in case a calm voice would affect the wolf. The glare didn't soften.

"Okay, we'll do this the hard way," said Clare. "Just don't bite me, okay?" She lowered herself completely onto the larger log, then knelt. This log too was covered with snow, but there were no branches to hold onto. She'd have to travel its length without anything to help her balance, so she'd be much safer crawling than walking, even though the snow was already numbing her hands.

She flipped the hackamore across her back so that it wouldn't get in the way as she crawled slowly along the log. A few feet from the glaring wolf, she stopped. She took the headstall from her shoulder, unclipped the single looped rein from the hackamore shank, then re-clipped it onto the same rein, making a loop like a lasso. Now, if she could just get the loop over the wolf's head and tighten it, she might be able to pull her along the front of the logjam and to shore.

The wolf was really struggling now. Terror slowly swallowed the rage in her eyes as if she could see her own death approaching. Her strength was failing and it was obvious that the poor thing couldn't last much longer.

Clare moved a bit farther along the log, pausing when she was almost within reach and made sure the loop was large enough to slip over the wolf's head. Then, holding it in her right hand and balancing herself with her left on the log, she leaned forward and threw the rein loop. It went over the wolf's head on the first try.

Stifling her triumph, Clare pulled gently on the rein – and instead of tightening, it slipped off the silver head.

The wolf was sinking even lower in the water and Clare knew she had just moments left. She glanced toward Angelica to see her bending over the two puppies, totally oblivious to the difficulties that Clare was having. And she was too far away to help now anyway.

Without help, there was only one thing she could do to save the wolf. She had to put the loop over the creature's head and tighten it with her hands. Would the wolf bite her? She looked so spent, as if every bit of her strength was gone. Surely she didn't have enough energy left to attack Clare.

Cautiously, the girl moved to the end of the log. Once again, rage battled with terror within the golden depths of the wolf's eyes. She tried to pull her lips back in a snarl, but was too low in the water and realized at the last moment that she couldn't open her mouth without choking.

Taking all her courage in hand, Clare leaned forward and flipped the loop over the wolf's head. Now she just had to tighten it – which meant her arm would be right beside the powerful jaws.

Dare she reach out? She had to if she was to save the

wolf. Taking a deep breath, Clare grabbed the leather rein with both hands and shoved the clip along its length. A strange moan came from the wolf when Clare's hand brushed against the course hair on her neck.

Clare jerked her hand away. She'd done it! Now she just had to pull the wolf along the logjam until it could get on shore. She crawled backward as far as she could while holding the headstall of the hackamore, then braced herself and pulled on the leather. The wolf's eyes widened as the noose tightened further around her neck, and for a moment, she struggled against the pull of the rein.

Clare clutched at the log with claw-like fingers, the hackamore headstall looped around her arm, and her heart pounding like crazy. The wolf had almost pulled her into the current! When the rein went slack, she looked up. The wolf was gone. Only the water boiled in front of Clare as the river was sucked beneath the logs.

"No!" she yelled and gave a mighty jerk on the leather. The mother wolf couldn't drown, not when her puppies needed her. Not when she'd tried so hard to survive.

Suddenly, the wolf thrashed to the surface, gasping and choking. She clawed at Clare's log, trying to climb up its wet and slippery surface.

Without hesitation, Clare shimmied back along the big log and pulled again. The wolf slid toward her, still struggling to climb out.

She loosened the tautness on the rein as she climbed up on the smaller log. She got her feet carefully beneath her, grasped the handy branch with one hand, and stood, then pulled again with the other hand. The wolf fought the rope again, pushed away from the log – and was once more sucked beneath the current.

Clare moved swiftly along the log. If she could just get to shore, she could pull harder on the hackamore. Within seconds, she jumped on the snow-covered ground and turned to stare at the river. She couldn't see the wolf, but took a firm hold on the leather of the hackamore and leaned back anyway. It was like pulling a massive fish from the water. The wolf felt like a dead weight on the end of the rein.

There she was, still below the surface but at least Clare could see her now. She backed a step, pulling the creature closer to shore. The wolf appeared to be unconscious. She wasn't even fighting anymore.

"Angelica! Come help!" She wasn't strong enough to pull the wolf up on the bank.

Something warm touched her shoulder.

"Smokey?"

The horse nickered behind her.

"Come in front of me, boy," she gasped. Her hands were slipping on the wet leather. She didn't want to let go, but unless she had help, she'd have no choice.

Thank goodness, the horse seemed to understand what she wanted. He stepped around her and squeezed between her and the edge of the river.

"Hold still, Smokes. I'm just going to put this around your neck, okay?"

Her fingers were too cold to undo the buckle to the headstall, so she wrapped the entire bundle of leather around the gelding's neck, then tied the thinner leather of the throatlatch around one of the thicker sidepieces. Slowly,

she let go. The headstall tightened around his neck, but didn't come undone.

"Okay, Smokes, now follow me. Quick." She stepped back.

Obediently, the gelding stepped after her. The headstall tightened further around his neck.

"Hurry, buddy. We don't want to choke you either." She rushed back a couple more steps and as the horse followed her, she peered around him. She could see the wolf's nose above the bank now, then the head – and then her body slid onto the snow.

"Whoa, Smokes. Good boy. Back up now." She pushed him on the chest and obediently he backed, then turned to look at the wolf.

She was unconscious. Or dead. Maybe Clare had been too slow.

"Take the rope off her neck before she wakes."

Clare turned to see Angelica standing behind Smokey, her hair stone white, the four puppies at her heels, all looking dry and healthy, but worried.

"Hurry. She is awakening."

With her heart in her throat, Clare crept toward the wolf. Her hands were so cold that she knew there was no way she would be able to undo the clip, but she could loosen the leather and slip it over the wolf's head – as long as she was fast enough. The wolf was already moving.

She reached down to grab the rein and pulled the clip along its length – and the yellow eyes opened, shining like two amber lights. Clare froze as the wolf's gaze bored into hers. Slowly, the lips pulled back into a snarl, showing white teeth just inches from her arm, a mere foot from her face.

Snowfall woke to see the human leaning over her, its face white with fear and cold and exhaustion.

It hadn't killed her. Instead it had pulled her to shore. It had saved her.

The human was touching the thing around her neck and she could feel its hands trembling. Snowfall growled, thinking to make the human move away. She had to get her feet beneath herself; she had to find her remaining puppies. It was too late for Scout and Aurora, and for that she would never forgive herself. She hadn't kept them safe. What was she thinking, leading them so close to the river? Of course the snow banks would be unstable there. She'd been lucky that only two of her puppies had fallen into the water.

She heard a puppy yip and moved her head to look. She must be mistaken. The yip had sounded like Scout.

And there he was, rushing toward her. And Aurora, Ice, and Tundra too. And there, in the willows, too afraid of the strange creatures to come forward, was Avalanche. They were all alive. How could it be?

There was a sharp tug around her neck and the hated thing slipped over her ears. Snowfall rolled upright as the human and caribou-creature hastily retreated, then groaned with satisfaction when her puppies tumbled over her. She felt their kisses on her muzzle and her ears rejoiced in the happy sounds of their reunion.

When she thought to look again for the human and her companions, the three of them were a fair distance away. They were making strange sounds to each other and watching Snowfall and her family with their teeth showing.

Clumsily, Snowfall climbed to her numb paws and took a step. She didn't fall, so she took another. Her strength was returning quickly. A miracle. Even more of a miracle was the health of Scout and Aurora. They seemed even stronger than they had before falling into the river.

She staggered to stand with Avalanche, the pups beside her, and together they looked back at the others. They were still watching.

Snowfall whined. The human had saved her, and had probably saved Scout and Aurora as well. It was the only explanation. So all humans weren't bad. She would avoid them in the future anyway, and teach her pups to do the same, because it was impossible to tell the good ones from the bad ones. But she no longer felt the burning hatred. Humans may have taken Ranger from them, but a human had also given her back two of her babies. She could forgive them, and be wary.

Avalanche disappeared into the willows, two of the pups at his heels. Snowfall pushed the last two to follow him, but before following herself, she turned back once more to look at the human, the caribou-creature, and the powerful one.

She would remember them, always. These three were safe.

Then she trotted into the willows. It was time to leave.

Clare turned to Angelica. "She's different. Did you see? She doesn't hate us anymore."

"She has forgiven us."

"For what?"

"She suffered a terrible tragedy, though I know not what."

"I can guess," Clare said, turning to Smokey. "A lot of people don't like wolves. I bet someone tried to shoot her or her puppies." She tugged on the mass of leather around the gelding's neck.

"Here, let me help. Your hands are too cold to free the headstall."

"Thanks." Clare stuffed her hands beneath her fleece top and gasped when they felt like icicles against her stomach. "Um, Angelica, I just wanted to say…" Angelica didn't look at her.

She isn't going to forgive me for being so mean to her, thought Clare. And how can I blame her?

She turned away and bit her lip as she stared across the rushing river. It didn't look nearly so dangerous from a few yards away.

I have to apologize anyway, she decided. It's up to Angelica if she forgives me. The only choice I have is to apologize or not, and she deserves an apology. I was mean to her.

"Angelica, I'm sorry."

"Sorry? What are you sorry for?" Angelica sounded genuinely puzzled.

Clare looked back to see the older girl slipping the untangled headstall on Smokey's head and re-clipping the rein to the shank.

"Well, I got so mad at you, and for hardly any reason. I just felt so horrible about leaving Smokey – I still feel that way – and so when you said to have faith, as if all I needed to do was believe that everything would be okay and then it would be, well, I just got mad." She looked down at the snow. "Especially after losing my dad. I thought like that then and it hurt so much when he didn't come home." She blinked away her tears as she looked up into Angelica's eyes. "But it doesn't matter how mad I was, I shouldn't have yelled at you. You were so nice to me. You saved me. You saved Smokey. And I'm really sorry."

"Oh Clare, *I* am sorry." Angelica's looked like she too was about to cry. "I did not mean it that way. I know faith cannot bring back your father. I know that forcing yourself to believe you and Smokey won't be separated won't make that come true."

"So what did you mean?"

"I meant to have faith in yourself to find ways to turn a terrible thing into something better, to choose the path that is not bitter but constructive." She reached out and touched Clare's hair. "Faith that *you* have the strength and power to turn a hard circumstance into something good."

"Really?"

"Yes, and I am so sorry that I did not explain myself better." Her hand dropped to her side.

Clare cleared her throat. "No more apologies, from either of us, okay?"

Angelica smiled.

"So you really think there's some way I can turn this into something good?" Clare asked her. "How?"

"I am not sure how, but there will be a way. If you think it through, you may come up with ideas or compromises that your mother can accept. Or possibly you could talk to your Mr. Davis to find a solution, since he is the one who decides Smokey's future." She turned to the horse. "He must understand that Smokey controls his own heart and his own loyalties. He must realize that Smokey desires to be with you."

"And I want to stay with him, more than anything. Do you really think I can do it? Convince them, I mean."

"If they are convince-able, then I believe you can convince them."

"And if they're not."

"You will find another way. I have faith in you, Clare, and so does Smokey. If you do not have enough for yourself, remember that *we* believe in you."

Clare looked deep into her horse's eyes. He did believe in her. He believed she could do anything. After saving the wolf, she almost believed it herself. "If you two have faith in me, then I do too," she said. "I'll find a way. Somehow."

Clare pulled Smokey to a halt at the mouth of the canyon and sighed as she stared across the tundra. It had been unbelievably hard to say goodbye to Angelica. Her hand went to her neck and she touched the stunning necklace that Angelica had created for her, magically, from a strand of her golden hair. She'd said that if Clare ever needed her, to touch the necklace and call her name and she would come. Then she'd added that if Clare needed more time to arrange to be with Smokey, she could shuffle messages back and forth between them.

Clare urged Smokey forward, her hand still on the golden chain. The warmth from it was uncanny but totally welcomed. It had heated her entire body almost instantly at the river and now was keeping her warm on her ride home.

Soon though, there would be no need for it. The flat land was sun-soaked. The temperature was climbing. Even the snow was getting patchy, though it still covered the ground inside the Chasm. Out here on the tundra, where the wind had blown it thin during the night, it was almost gone. Vibrant brush colored the landscape and lemmings scuttled beneath their cover. Smokey flushed out a rabbit as he walked and snorted as its brown and white rear dashed away from them.

Clare sighed with contentment and her hand touched the necklace again. Angelica, a magical, wonderful being, had faith in her. Angelica, who could do almost anything, thought that Clare could do the same. Angelica, who Clare was now sure had seen countless tragedies and trials, still remained kind and full of hope… The thought made her feel tingly all over. Somehow she'd convince her mom to come back north next year.

"Clare!"

The call came from far away and the girl reined in Smokey and shaded her eyes to peer to the horizon. Two riders approached at a quick lope. Though they were still far away she recognized Queenie, the chestnut mare that her mom rode most of the time, and Elvis, Mr. Davis's flashy pinto. Clare waved, then encouraged Smokey to trot toward them.

When the three horses came together, Clare's mom launched off of the chestnut's back and ran toward Clare and Smokey, reaching up to hug Clare before she'd even dismounted. Clare slid from Smokey's back and hugged her mom hard.

"We thought… we thought the worst," her mom said in one breath. "We couldn't see how you could survive the blizzard. Oh, Clare." Tears streamed down her cheeks.

"Mom, Mom, I'm okay. Really. I found a cave and stayed there the whole time. There were no problems, or nothing I couldn't handle. I even had a fire to keep warm." None of her words were lies, she reasoned, though they didn't exactly tell the whole truth either. But she'd promised Angelica she wouldn't say anything about her, so she had no choice but to be evasive.

"Oh sweetie, I am so sorry."

"No, Mom. I'm sorry. I was the one who ran off." Clare pulled away a bit and stared into her mom's eyes – eyes that were red from crying, because of her. "I was the one who didn't stay home and talk about it. I was the one who came to the Chasm even though I knew I wasn't allowed."

"And thank goodness you did," said Mr. Davis. "If you'd been out in the open, I don't know how you could have survived the storm."

"How did you find me, anyway?"

"Well, I saw you heading this direction yesterday, so I was suspicious," said Mr. Davis.

"But it was more than that," added Clare's mom. "Queenie and Elvis seemed to know where to go. They brought us straight to you."

Clare smiled. More of Angelica's magic, she'd wager. "Mom, we need to talk."

"I know, honey. Why don't we talk on the ride home?" Then she pulled Clare into another hug. "I'm just so glad you're safe. I still can't believe it." She sounded like she was going to cry again.

"It was an adventure," said Clare, her voice muffled by her mom's shoulder. "I wanted an adventure before I left."

"Well," drawled Mr. Davis, "you certainly got one."

Reluctantly, Clare's mom released her and boosted her to Smokey's back. Then she mounted Queenie and the three of them started toward home. After a few seconds of silence, Mr. Davis said, "I think I'll go on ahead and make sure there's something ready to eat when you get home."

Clare's mom nodded gratefully and Clare's stomach rumbled at the thought of food. She was famished.

When Mr. Davis and Elvis were out of earshot, Clare's mom sighed. "I know you're upset about leaving, honey. I know you love the north."

"I think we should come back next spring."

"That's impossible. Mr. Davis is retiring and selling the ranch."

Clare felt her heart sink. That meant that Smokey would be sold along with the rest of the horses, probably to whoever bought the ranch. There was no way she could afford to buy him right now. Even if she saved for years, his new owner might not want to sell him. Horses that were careful with beginner riders were almost worth their weight in gold.

But Angelica said to have faith in myself, she remembered. There must be some way.

"What do you think about getting a job in Whitehorse next summer? That way we could come back and stay." And I'll be able to visit Smokey, she added in her head.

"I've already got another job, in the Okanogan, as head chef in a nice restaurant. It's something I've always wanted, Clare." She sounded like she was begging her daughter to understand. "I think you'll be happy there. It's a nice little town and we can stay there year round instead of moving every six months. You could make friends and you wouldn't miss the last weeks of school every year. You could do activities and join sports teams. It'll be a normal life for us, for a change."

"But I like the way things are."

"You'll like the other too, believe me. You've just never had it, so you don't know."

"But…"

"Please, honey, try to understand."

Clare bit her lip. How was she going to convince her mom to come back up here? It seemed impossible. All her mom could see were the positive things about settling down.

"But if we moved up here and didn't leave in the winter, I could still have all those things."

"But my new job, it's such an opportunity and I don't want to lose it. Besides, it's awfully cold in the winter up here, and dark. I don't know if you'd like it."

"I'm sure I would, especially if I could visit Smokey. He's the one I'll miss more than anything."

A puzzled look crept across her mom's face. "But wouldn't you rather have him down south? It's so much nicer to ride year round there. You could even see if he likes to show, or jump, or do gymkhana."

Clare inhaled sharply. "You mean…" For some reason the words couldn't come.

"What?"

"…I can take him with me?" she whispered.

"Oh honey, didn't you hear me yesterday? I called after you and I thought you'd heard."

Could it be true? Could her mom be saying what Clare hoped she was saying?

"Mr. Davis has given Smokey to you. He's yours. We'll be taking him with us. We can't always control how much time we have with those we love, but when we can –"

"Oh, Mom!" Tears burst from Clare's eyes and she couldn't do anything but throw her arms around her very own horse's neck. He was hers! Smokey was hers!

Smokey stopped and nickered, then turned his head and touched her leg with his warm muzzle. Clare hiccupped as she fought from being carried away by her tears, and then she felt Queenie brush against her and her mom's hand rubbing her back. She was saying something too, but Clare couldn't hear her words. Her mind was shouting too loudly with relief. She wouldn't have to leave her Smokey. They wouldn't be parted.

She touched the necklace's warm, tingling length. Everything's okay, she thought.

*I am so glad,* Angelica's voice spoke in her mind. *I knew you could do it.*

Despite her tears, Clare smiled. She hadn't done anything except listen. And next time she'd do the same – she'd listen and not storm off before all their words were said.

Thanks, she thought to Angelica. Thanks so much for everything.

Though Angelica was silent, Clare felt her smile like a warm light around her. Then the girl's presence was gone.

"Are you alright, honey?" Her mom sounded so worried. "It's what you want, isn't it? To bring Smokey with you?"

Clare straightened on her horse's back and rubbed her tears away, not caring if dirty streaks remained on her face. She didn't care about anything right now, except that Smokey was going with them. "We'll miss the north," she said to her mom, her voice full of feeling. "But really, the best thing about being here is Smokey. If I can take him…" Emotion choked off her words again and Smokey filled the silence with his throaty nicker.

"My two babies," said Clare's mom. "Or should I say three. Queenie is coming too. Mr. Davis gave them both to us as a thank you for all our years up here. And Queenie is close to retirement. She'll need a good home."

"Mr. Davis so nice."

"That he is," agreed her mom.

"But we deserve them too," added Clare, her voice stronger.

Her mom smiled. "That we do." She asked Queenie to walk and Smokey strode along beside her.

"And we'll take perfect care of them. They'll live to be ancient horses who are so loved and cuddled, that they'll break the world record because they'll live so long and so happily."

Clare's mom laughed. "That they will." Then she gasped and pulled Queenie to a quick stop. "Look, Clare."

Another mountain bluebird swooped down in front of them and landed on a bush. Its warble flowed around them and its sky blue wings flashed beneath the sun.

"I saw one yesterday too," Clare whispered.

"The last time I saw one was ages ago, when we came up north the first time. Your dad and I went for a walk on the tundra and one swooped out of the sky, just like this fellow, and sang for us."

"You still miss him, don't you, Mom?"

"Yes, I do, and I probably always will." Her voice was so soft that Clare hardly heard her. "But I have you, Clare. And we have Mr. Davis and other good friends like him and our horses. And I have faith that even the hardest situations can bring good things."